CHARLES D HALE

Harrison Undercover

The Sherriff Harrison Saga Vol 2

Some of our authors do participate in speaking arrangements. If interested, please visit the website below.
www.sillygoatmedia.com

Library of Congress Cataloging-in-Publication Data
Charles D Hale –
Harrison Undercover: The Sheriff Harrison Saga Vol 2
First Edition: August 2026

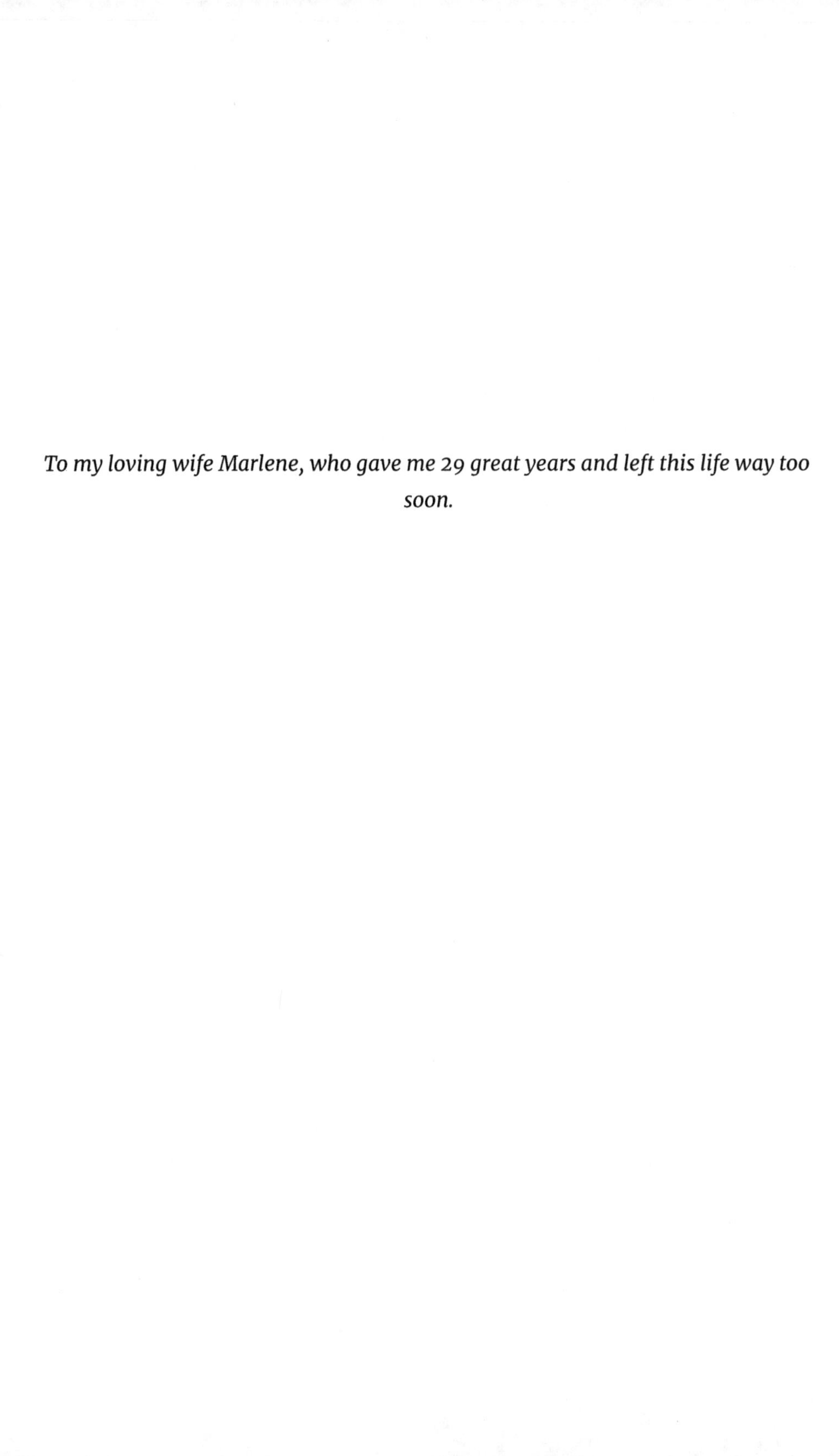

To my loving wife Marlene, who gave me 29 great years and left this life way too soon.

Contents

CHAPTER 1

The portable radio in my jacket pocket squawked and a garbled voice said, "I think I see something." It was Dan Dawson, one of my part-time deputies. He was about as laid-back as they come, but I couldn't ask for a better man in a tough situation, and I had learned to appreciate his droll sense of humor. He was teamed up with Bruce Johnson, my Chief Deputy. They were positioned three miles east of my location, on a bluff overlooking the highway.

A bitter-cold wind rushed in from the north bringing a promise of snow. I was alone, snuggled into my down-lined jacket, crouched behind a fallen juniper tree, and squinted into the infrared binoculars, focused on a small herd of cattle about 200 yards away. Heavy clouds played hide and seek with a half moon and stood in faint relief against the ink-black sky. From my perch on a rocky knoll, I had a commanding view of the valley in all directions and I waited with nervous anticipation for the rustlers to appear.

Dawson and Johnson were about as different as night and day, but they made a good combination. Bruce was amiable, slow-talking and mild-mannered, but absolutely dependable. He was the rock I'd hired to help me run the department, and he hadn't let me down. Dawson, on the other hand, was a young go-getter who needed to be restrained from time to time. He had a good head on his shoulders, but he sometimes lacked the judgment that only comes with experience.

I'd hired Bruce shortly after being sworn in as the new Sheriff of El Dorado County in Climax, Colorado. He had approached me several days after I'd taken over as sheriff. Bruce had been a police officer in Omaha and had quit because he grew sick of the politics that went with the job. He moved to the area to farm, but missed the excitement of police work. Only problem was, police work in a small town in El Dorado County, which was mostly rural in character, was usually not very exciting. But that was about to change.

When Bruce asked me about a job, I made a quick assessment and decided that he might be the ideal person to take over my spot as Chief Deputy since there was no one in the ranks who had the experience I needed. While we didn't always agree, I had learned to trust and respect him, and our skills complemented one another. It had turned out to be a good decision.

Another disembodied voice barked over the portable radio. "I make out two vehicles heading your way. Can you pick them up yet, Dan?" This was Steve Jordan, our local State Trooper – a prize-winning rodeo star turned patrolman – who was posted farther east on the highway.

"Yeah, we got 'em," Dan drawled. "Pickup truck followed by a large cattle truck. They're turnin' onto the service road headin' south. Comin' yer way, Sheriff."

A surge of excitement raced down my spine as I pressed the "talk" button on the radio. "I read you, Dan. You copy, Henry?"

Henry Raven's gravely voice replied, "Copy here." Henry was the Chief of the Sequoia Indian Tribal Police. We were actually on the Sequoia Indian reservation, most of which is in El Dorado County. Indian reservations are considered sovereign territories by federal law and only tribal police or federal officers have jurisdiction over offenses committed on them. Raven had requested us to assist his tribal police due to his own lack of manpower. It was Henry's show, but we were here to help him put a bunch of modern-day cattle rustlers out of business.

I peered into the night-vision binoculars again and spotted two shapes moving quickly through the darkness toward me. "I have them now," I said into the radio. "They're about three hundred yards from the target. All posts maintain your position."

A series of electronic squawks signaled acknowledgment. I was no longer aware of the cold. The trap had been set and was about to be sprung.

"All hands, copy, maintain your positions," Henry commanded. He was positioned in a grove of trees a hundred yards south of me. Between us, the small herd of cattle slept, undisturbed by the bitter cold wind. This was the target, and it was just a matter of minutes before the long, uncomfortable nights of waiting and watching would yield results.

"Steve, what's your position?" Henry asked.

"About a half-mile east of you, Henry," Jordan replied.

"All units," Henry said, "give them five minutes to start loading, then head in on my signal."

Several squawks were heard on the radio as we all acknowledged Henry's command.

I enjoyed working with Raven and his men but the relationship between our two forces hadn't always been so cordial. My predecessor was a fine lawman but didn't have much use for the tribal police and tried to keep as much distance as possible between them and his own department. Soon after taking over as sheriff, I realized that we had too much in common to remain isolated from each other and that we could accomplish more by joining forces.

Jim Jenkins, the former sheriff, would not have approved of our current arrangement, but I was the one getting paid to make those decisions now.

When Henry Raven came to me to request assistance in tracking down the persons responsible for a series of cattle thefts on the reservation, I wasn't sure this was something the Sheriff's Office should get involved in. But when he explained that the well-organized thefts were threatening the livelihood of some of the ranchers who leased their land from the Tribal Council, I agreed to help the tribal police on what I considered a matter of mutual interest. I called the commander of the state patrol in our area and he agreed to lend a hand as well.

Working together, we studied every reported theft of cattle for the previous two years and began looking for patterns and similarities. All of the thefts occurred during the hours of darkness in remote places where discovery would be unlikely. We suspected that the thieves were using one or two large trucks or tractor trailers capable of carrying up to fifty head of cattle each. The thieves moved in quickly and used back roads and the cover of darkness to avoid detection. We theorized that the thieves transported the stolen cattle to an out-of-state processing plant where the operators weren't too choosy about ownership papers or bills of sale.

We developed a profile of the thefts and put together a list of every site in the county that might fit. We eventually were able to identify three sites that most closely matched this description and developed a surveillance plan for each one. We elected to spend three nights at each site and hoped that our plan would work. Our first two sites didn't pan out, but it looked as if we were about to hit pay dirt on the third one.

The radio squawked again. "They've arrived," said Michael Dove, Henry's lone deputy. Michael was a large, quiet man and was an unlikely candidate for a lawman, but as loyal and dedicated as could be. I had met his older sister, Mona Dove, during a previous encounter involving the treacherous and cunning leader of the Sequoia Tribal Council, B. J. Tall Horse, who was now safely locked up in prison serving a life sentence for murder and other assorted crimes. I respected Mona Dove for her courage and wisdom, and I had come to know that her brother possessed the same qualities.

Henry keyed the radio and said, "Michael, are you getting this on tape?"

The radio crackled back and he replied, "We are live and rolling!"

Nothin' but high tech out here on the western slopes, I chucked to myself.

My night-vision binoculars brought the scene below into sharp focus. Two trucks turned off the road and headed to where the unsuspecting cattle slept. I watched as two men jumped out of the late-model F-150 pickup truck. Two more men climbed down from the cab of the cattle truck, and all four got busy, workin' as a well-rehearsed team.

After dropping a ramp from the bed of the cattle truck, one man put a noose over the neck of a sleeping cow while a second rustler using an electric cattle rod to get the animal on its feet and moving to the ramp and into the transport truck. The second two-man team followed suit.

It was obvious they'd done this before, but the show was about to come to a dramatic end.

"All units," Henry announced, "the suspects are loading the cattle.

Move in ... now!"

Steve Jordan acknowledged, "I'm on my way."

I was the closest. I ran to my cruiser, turned on the ignition, threw on my headlights, bringing the scene into bright illumination. Using my PA system,

I shouted, "This is Sheriff Clint Harrison of El Dorado County. You men are under arrest for cattle rustling. Don't move!"

Quicker than I thought possible, three of the men dashed toward the pickup truck and got into the cab. The fourth drew a revolver from a holster and snapped off three rounds in my direction before diving into the bed of the pickup truck, which was already racing toward a nearby access road. One round took out my left headlight, but the others went astray. I took cover behind my dash, then grabbed my radio and warned the others that the suspects were armed and attempting to flee.

Bruce Johnson's low drawl announced that he and Dan were headed in my direction, while I took off after the thieves who had a good head start.

"All units, all units," I shouted into the microphone. "Suspects are north-bound on the access road approximately one mile west of the highway. Henry, are you in a position to cut them off?"

"Negative, sheriff, but I'm headin' in that direction. I'll need a minute or two."

By the time I reached the access road, the thieves were nearly a quarter mile ahead of me and pulling away rapidly. I pressed harder on the accelerator and the old Buick lunged forward, shimmying wildly on the uneven surface of the road.

"Bruce, I'm being shot at and can't get too close. I'll have to tail them from a safe distance. See if you can parallel us northbound on the highway. They may try to cut back in your direction."

"Roger that."

I could barely hear him over the roar of the engine.

"Sheriff, we may have a problem," Steve Jordan announced. "What's that?" I replied. I was having enough trouble trying to keep my car on the rut-filled road and talk into the mike at the same time.

"They've closed the highway three miles north of here for resurfacing," he replied. "I'll have to detour to Coyote Junction and that'll cost me a good ten minutes."

"Do the best you can, Steve. I'll try to stay with them, but I'll need backup. Henry, do you copy?"

"I copy. I'm gonna take that service road we just passed."

That left only me to follow until we got them corralled. I gripped the steering wheel firmly, doing my best to keep the Buick on the uneven surface of the road, while slowly increasing my speed.

I was able to keep he rustlers in sight, but the guy in the bed of the pickup truck was determined to pick me off and fired another volley in my direction. The wild careening of the pickup made it impossible for him to shoot accurately, and his shots missed their mark.

I was content to keep them in view and wait for backup. I radioed my position to Steve Jordan, hoping he' be in position to intercept the thieves.

"You should be just about to the old highway maintenance road, Sheriff," he replied. "They may be planning on taking that back to the main highway. But if they don't, they're in for a surprise."

"What's that?" I asked.

"That road hasn't been used in years and the bridge is out at White Water Canyon. If they try to cross over, they're going to get wet!"

I smiled at the thought of the pickup truck flying through space into the river below.

The road angled sharply to the right and I spun the wheel hard. Too late, I saw the trunk of a dead tree directly in my path and I winced as the car glanced off the tree with a sickening thud. I punched the accelerator and the heavy car lunged forward, but a shudder in the front end told me that the steering system had probably been damaged.

By the time I reached the old maintenance road, I knew it would be only seconds before the driver of the truck realized too late that the bridge was out. But I needed backup if I was to have a chance of capturing the thieves. On foot, four of them could scatter in all directions, making good their escape.

"Henry, I'm heading east on the old maintenance road. How far away are you?"

After a pause, he said, "We're less than a mile out. We'll get there pronto."

Bruce Johnson radioed, "Sheriff, we're headin' your way comin' in from the east on a service road. We're about two minutes out."

I acknowledged, feeling relieved. If the thieves abandoned their vehicle, we'd have them fairly well boxed in. Now the odds were leaning in our favor.

The thieves topped the crest of a small hill and were plummeting down the grade on the other side. But, to my surprise, rather than slowing down, they were accelerating, and I realized that they were going to try to make it across the bridge. They had apparently chosen to ignored the warning approach signs, and decided to take their chances.

The driver of the truck realized his mistake too late. He entered what was left of the abandoned bridge, then tried to stop, his brake lights glaring in the darkness. Tires screeched in protest as the truck hurtled violently through the barricades, then crashed through a twisted guard rail, and tumbled into the dark waters below. The rustler in the bed of the truck leaped at the last second and landed in a lifeless heap just beyond the mangled guard rail.

I stopped just short of the barricade and ran to check on the one who'd been thrown clear, but he wasn't going anywhere. A quick check indicated that his neck had been broken. I recovered his empty revolver a few feet from where he lay.

At that moment, Steve Jordan arrived and we ran to the bridge and watched as the partially submerged pickup truck was carried away by the swiftly moving current.

I keyed the radio and said, "Henry, try to get down river in case any of the thieves manage to get ashore." Given the rapid current below, it was unlikely that any of the thieves would survive, but we needed to be ready if they did.

"We're about a quarter mile south of you Clint, down by where the river narrows some," Henry replied. "How many are we looking for?"

"Three, Henry," I replied. "Number four is here with me and not going anywhere.

Steve Jordan ran back to his patrol car and said, "I'll get on down there and give them a hand."

I called back to my dispatcher and requested paramedics in the unlikely event that we recovered any survivors.

Michael Dove's excited voice came on the radio. "Sheriff, we have the vehicle in sight. It's fully submerged and hung up on a dead tree branch near the shore."

I waited for a progress report. Finally, Henry came on the radio. "We'll need some help on this, Clint. At least two are trapped inside, both DOA, but no sign of a third."

"Roger that," I replied, then contacted our dispatcher again. "Paula, we need the county's underwater recovery team out here as quick as they can come, and you need to call Doc Underwood, the coroner, too."

Just then, Steve Jordan radioed, "I've got the last one here, Sheriff.

He's near drowned, but alive."

"Roger that, Steve, I'll get EMS on their way. What's your location?"

He gave me his position and I called Paula back and told her where to send the paramedics, then added, "Make sure we have a deputy at the hospital ER to take charge of the prisoner once EMS delivers him there. I want him booked on attempted cattle rustling just as soon as he arrives. Also, you'd better tell highway maintenance about the situation here at the bridge. They've got a bit of cleanup to do."

The first light of day was beginning to peek over the mountains to the east and for the first time in hours I had a chance to relax and take stock of our situation. It certainly hadn't turned out the way I'd expected, but I'd been in law enforcement long enough to know that even the best laid plans rarely work out exactly the way they're drawn up. But we'd stopped the thieves in their tracks, no cattle had been lost, none of our people had been hurt, and one of the thieves was in custody.

It had been a long night, and I was feeling the strain of fatigue, but I still had work to do. I was anxious to question the survivor in the hope of clearing up the other rustling cases that had occurred in the area. It was unfortunate that his three companions had lost their lives, but I hoped this would put an end to cattle rusting in El Dorado County.

CHAPTER 2

Two days after the cattle rustling incident, I arrived at work early to get caught up on the paperwork that would be needed for court the following day. After his release from the hospital, the surviving cattle rustler had been booked into our jail and Lilly Martinez, our lead investigator, had managed to obtain a full confession from him about the group's recent thefts. He'd be arraigned the following morning, and I told Lilly to make sure she'd be available to confer with the county prosecutor if he had any questions. She assured me that she'd be there.

The intercom on my desk squawked, rudely interrupting my thoughts, and I nearly spilled the cup of steaming coffee that I had yet to drink. I made a mental note to ask Myra to see if there wasn't some other tone that could be found to replace the harsh sound of the intercom. Maybe something like soft chimes?

"What is it, Myrna?" I glanced at the clock on the wall – it was only seven-thirty in the morning, a little early for any official calls.

I waited for an answer; instead, Myrna Henderson – mid-fifties, trim, with blonde hair growing grey, wearing a white blouse and knee-length blue skirt – entered my office, closed the door behind her, then pushed her back against it as if she were expecting vandals to come bursting in. Her face was flushed and her eyes were wide with either fear or excitement. It turned out to be the latter.

"On line one, Sheriff. It's Nelson Bradford!" She expelled the words breathlessly, as if she needed to get them out before they exploded in her throat. It took me a moment to comprehend who she meant, then I understood her excitement.

"You're referring to Nelson Bradford, the ..." I knew who, or rather what, Nelson Bradford was, but I couldn't fathom why he'd be calling me.

She nodded three times in succession, struggling to contain her excitement. "He's Governor Franklin's Chief of Staff, and he wants to speak with you!"

I had to admit that I was curious about this early morning call. What in the devil could Bradford want with me? Must be some kind of political fund-raiser, I decided, and my mood changed from curiosity to annoyance. Even though I'm technically an "elected official", I was appointed to the office because the death of the former sheriff left me as the logical successor, but I've never considered myself much of a politician.

Myrna glanced nervously at the telephone on my desk and her eyes implored me to take the call before the telephone mysteriously disappeared into thin air. She made no move to leave, clearly more curious about the nature of the call than I was.

I picked up the receiver. "Hello, Mr. Bradford. This is Sheriff Harrison. How may I help you?"

I'd met Nelson Bradford briefly two months ago at the dedication of the new State Law Enforcement Training Center in Capitol City. He'd been there representing the governor and I recalled the power and authority that seemed to ooze from every pore in his body. He impressed me as a man who knew his way around and who was used to being in charge. While he might lack the formal authority of the governor, it was obvious that he had the ability to move mountains if necessary to get what he wanted. As the governor's chief of staff, Bradford was the primary source of political clout behind Governor Howard Franklin, who might still be a county commissioner in diminutive Laredo County if it hadn't been for the political know-how and financial connections of Nelson Bradford. He was without a doubt the man behind the throne, and a force to be reckoned with in his own right.

"Sheriff Harrison! How are things in El Dorado County?" Bradford's voice was low and strong, suggesting the same self-confidence and "take charge" attitude he projected in person.

"Quiet, Mr. Bradford," I said. "Just the way we like it here. How are things in Capitol City?"

Myrna stood by, fidgeting nervously, waiting for some sign from me, but I gave her none.

"Let me get right to the point, Sheriff Harrison," Bradford went on.

The floor was all his, and we both knew it.

"The governor is interested in discussing a matter of some, ah, sensitivity with you, Sheriff Harrison." Before I could respond, he added, "It's something he'd rather discuss with you face to face."

His words caught me off guard. Bradford's voice was very serious when he mentioned a matter of "sensitivity", and I couldn't imagine anything that would necessitate the need to speak in person.

He didn't wait for my reply. "Would tomorrow afternoon, say around three o'clock, fit into your schedule, Sheriff Harrison?"

"Tomorrow afternoon, Mr. Bradford?" I gazed at Myrna, who told me in exaggerated sign language that I had no appointments that couldn't be rescheduled.

"Why, I suppose I can work that in. It's about a four-hour drive from here to Capitol City, so I can –"

"No need, Sheriff," Bradford cut in. "There's a private landing strip three miles west of Climax. I'll meet you there with the governor's plane at two o'clock tomorrow afternoon. It's only a thirty-five-minute flight from there to Capitol City. I'll have you back in Climax in time for dinner."

Bradford had my itinerary completely organized, and a short flight to the state capitol and back beat spending eight hours on the road through a few hundred miles of sagebrush, cactus and pinion trees. I told Bradford that I'd meet him at the landing strip at two o'clock; he thanked me and hung up.

I sat there thinking about the call, and realized that I had no better idea of why he had called than I had before the conversation began.

Myrna was beside herself with excitement. She reacted to the call as if I'd been invited to dine with the Queen of England.

"He's sending his private plane to pick you up?" Myrna said breathlessly. "My gosh, I can't believe it! Did he say what the governor wants with you? I bet he wants to appoint you to some high-level cabinet job or something. Oh, darn it all, just when things were going good around here, you take off and get some fancy job up in Capitol City." She had it all figured out, and her mood turned from excitement to disappointment in seconds.

I tried to act casual, as if I was used to being invited to meet the governor on a regular basis, but I couldn't conceal my own bewilderment – and a little excitement – about the invitation I'd just received.

"I have no idea, Myrna, but I'm sure it's something quite routine. Governor

Franklin is a strong 'law and order' man, and it's not unusual for him to ask for advice from law enforcement administrators on various issues being discussed in the legislature. He probably just wants to get my opinion on some particular issue."

She screwed up her face as if she'd just eaten a sour lemon. "Oh, I'm sure that's it. That's why he had his chief of staff call you at 7:30 in the morning to talk to you. And that's why he's sending his personal plane down to pick you up. Probably something very 'routine', all right." She laughed sarcastically, then opened the door and returned to her desk.

I spent the next hour at my desk, forcing myself to attend to the paperwork that had piled up over the weekend, but my mind was miles away, thinking about the next day's meeting with the governor. What could the governor possible want with the sheriff of a rural county in the southwestern corner of the state – someone with only six months on the job?

I thought about this and swung my chair around to stare out the window at the majestic vista of stately, snow-clad mountain peaks that sprawled across the eastern horizon. It was hard to believe that I'd drifted into the town of Climax only a year ago, trying to escape the tortuous memory of the tragic deaths of my wife and young son. I'd unwittingly gotten mixed up in a criminal conspiracy involving the leader of the local Indian tribe. Because of my previous experience as an Assistant District Attorney in Southern California, Sheriff Jenkins had convinced me to take on an undercover assignment to investigate a series of unusual events that had resulted in the near-fatal accident involving the local newspaper publisher. Ultimately, through sheer luck, I was able to unravel the mystery and bring the culprits to justice. The dramatic conclusion of the episode drew national attention and gained me a bit of notoriety in the state.

Afterwards, Sheriff Jenkins offered me a position as Chief Deputy, and for the first time since leaving Southern California, my life started to make sense.

Unfortunately, only three months after swearing me in as the number two man in the department, Sheriff Jenkins died of a massive coronary while on a fishing trip on Deer Lake. Knowing how much Jim Jenkins loved the outdoors in general and fishing in particular, at least he'd left this life enjoying what he was doing.

It wasn't a huge surprise when the County Commissioners informed me that they intended to appoint me as the interim sheriff until the next general election, two years later. I had no real interest in the job, and had never wanted to become a political figure, but they correctly pointed out that there was no one else in the department with any kind of professional training or administrative experience. I had no plans to leave Climax anytime soon, so I agreed to serve the remainder of Jim Jenkins' term of office.

Now, a year later, I had to admit that I was beginning to enjoy my new role. I'd started out as a cop in one of the small beach towns in Southern California after serving a four-year hitch in the Marine Corps. I loved being a cop. The pay was good and I became pretty good at it.

An added benefit was that it was a particularly good way for a single young man to meet single young women. It was, in fact, how I had met Janet, who I fell in love with the day I stopped to help her fix a flat tire on her car. She insisted on thanking me by buying me lunch. One thing led to another and six months later we were married. It was, we both thought, a union made in heaven.

Janet encouraged me to go back to school; four years later, I graduated from law school at USC. I applied for a position with the Los Angeles County District Attorney's office. My background in police work was a plus as I traded in my gun belt for a briefcase, but I knew I was still in the business of putting criminals behind bars, and that made it all worthwhile.

Shortly after I joined the DA's office Janet became pregnant. My son Jason was my pride and joy, next to Janet, who I loved more than life itself. The loss of them in a car bomb intended for me, planted by a drug cartel that I'd been prosecuting, left a void in my soul that I didn't think would ever be filled.

The awful buzzing of the intercom interrupted my thoughts for the second time that morning, and Myrna said, "Sheriff, it's Ms. Newsome. Are you available?"

There was a coldness to her voice that reminded me of her resentment toward the woman who currently occupied a central place in my life. I didn't know why, but I suspected that there may have been bad blood between the two women long before I came into the picture, but I knew enough not to discuss it with either of them.

I'd met Mary Alice Newsome, who worked as a waitress at The Main Street Café shortly after my arrival in town, and she had given my life new meaning. We'd developed strong feelings for each other – maybe not love, but something close – and we were content to take things one day at a time. I wasn't sure exactly where the relationship was headed, but the emotional attachment between us was strong. I cared deeply for her, and I believed she felt the same way about me. I needed someone like her in my life, and she seemed to feel the same way about me.

Mary Alice had a previous relationship that hadn't ended well, and she still suffered from the pain that comes with being the victim of physical and mental abuse. I couldn't imagine what she'd been through, but I wanted to do my best to make her happy. We enjoyed being together, knowing that the future would take care of itself. If and when the time came for us to take our relationship to another level, we'd be ready to do just that.

I picked up the receiver. "Hi," I said, eager to hear her voice. "Hi back. What are you doing?"

I could imagine Mary Alice in her apartment, lounging around in jeans and a blouse with her hair tied above her head in a way that left her beautiful neck exposed and enticing. I had an impulse to leave the paperwork behind and rush to her apartment, but I managed to restrain myself.

"Oh, the usual – arrest reports, complaints, calls from the governor's office – you know."

"What? A call from the governor's office?" she echoed, her voice raising an octave or two.

I told her about the call from Nelson Bradford and tried to downplay its importance, but she didn't buy it.

"From what little I know about Nelson Bradford," she said, her words dripping with sarcasm, "I don't think I would trust him any farther than I could throw him!"

I laughed at her choice of words. She had a healthy disdain for politicians and I couldn't blame her.

"I'm sure the governor just wants to talk with me about that new Crime Control Bill that's being debated in the legislature," I replied calmly. "Rumor has it that he has some reservations about the bill and is seeking advice from some of the law enforcement heads in the state. He may simply want my input." I didn't believe that for a minute, and I knew she probably wouldn't either, but it was worth a try.

The snort on the other end of the line was not very ladylike, and let me know that she wasn't buying it, any more than Myrna had.

"Clint, my darling, you know I love you, but you'll have to come up with a better line than that. It wouldn't have worked the day I met you and it certainly won't work now!"

She could read me like a book, but it was one of the things I loved about her.

"Actually, my love," I said, deciding to play it straight with her, "I don't have a clue as to why the governor wants to see me. Or why it's so urgent that he's sending Bradford down here on his private jet to escort me to meet the governor. I'm totally in the dark on this one, but I have to admit I'm intrigued by the idea that the governor considers me that important."

"Well," she replied, scolding me gently, "whatever he is selling, I just hope you won't decide to buy until you know the actual price."

I laughed again at her skepticism, even though I knew she was right. "You mean you think he may not just be giving something away and he's chosen me because I'm his favorite county sheriff?"

It was her turn to laugh. The sound was sweet enough to turn stone into sugar.

"Well, my darling," she said seriously, "will I see you tonight?" "Who's going to keep me away?"

I replied playfully. "What time do you get off work?

"I'm scheduled till six, but it may be a little later. The new girl I'm breaking in is taking a while to get the hang of things, and Sherman may want me to stay with her awhile longer."

"Not a problem. Why don't I come by the café around six-thirty and have coffee until you're ready to leave?"

She said that would be fine and whispered goodbye in a way that made me wish she was sitting next to me so that I could smell the sweet lilac scent of her perfume. But I had more than enough to keep me busy until 6:30. But, as I did my best to keep busy, my thoughts kept drifting back to my conversation with Bradford. And I couldn't escape the feeling that my meeting with the governor would be anything but routine.

CHAPTER 3

Main Street Café was one of the more popular eating restaurants in Climax, and it is generally known for its good food, generous portions, reasonable prices, and speedy service. That's where I first met Mary Alice shortly after coming to town.

She was a waitress and, I can honestly say, the best one there. While my opinion may be slightly influenced by the fact that I am totally devoted to her, I truly believe that she's the epitome of charm, efficiency and hard work.

It was nearly 6:30 by the time I arrived. The place was teeming with customers and nearly every table was full. I took a seat at the counter and caught Mary Alice's eye as she emerged through the swinging doors from the kitchen carrying a large tray. The look she returned told me that it might be a while before she was able to leave. I ordered a cup of coffee from Sherman, the afternoon manager, who was working the counter and register.

Sherman poured me a cup, then leaned toward me, resting his elbows on the counter.

"Heard ya had some excitement last night out at the reservation, Sheriff."

By now the news of the attempted cattle theft and the resulting fatal accident was all over the county. Sherman hadn't been the only one to approach me, hoping to hear the gory details, but I had no interest in discussing official business with him.

Sherman Reynolds was a tall, angular man, whose age I guessed to be somewhere on the far side of seventy. He had shaggy hair the color of molasses that seemed to be in a constant state of disarray. His face was long and etched with more wrinkles than I could count, and his eyes drooped on either side, making him look sad despite his usual upbeat personality. His nose was two sizes too large for the rest of his face, and he always seemed to be blowing it into a large red handkerchief that he kept wadded up into his hip pocket. He had the largest hands I had ever seen on a human being, and I imaged that he could easily pick up a basketball in one hand.

The fingers of his right hand were tobacco stained and he reeked of cigarette smoke. He once told me that he still smoked two packs of Camel cigarettes a day; and yet he seemed as healthy as a man two decades younger. It just proves that there are no absolutes in life and that for every rule there will be an exception.

Sherman had an encyclopedic memory which, coupled with his vast knowledge of the town and all who lived in it, made him an invaluable source of information. As far as I was concerned, he ranked right up there with the Yellow Page, the Thomas Street Guide and the American edition of Who's Who as a source of useful information. But Sherman was also the town's biggest gossip, which was why I had no intention of sharing anything with him that I didn't want everyone in town to know as well.

"Not a whole lot to tell, Sherman," I said, looking straight into his soulful brown eyes, and knowing full well that he could see right through my lie.

"In other words, you can't talk about it, right Sheriff?" "Yep, Sherman, you're right on the money."

He nodded silently but I knew he wasn't going to give up that easily. He continued to rest his arms on the counter and made no effort to move, as if it was his preferred position of repose. "Them fellas that were killed, I heard they were from up by Junction City. They gotta record, Sheriff?"

I gave him my best No comment stare, but he didn't even blink. He was like a bloodhound, hot on the trail of any juicy tidbits I might happen to discard; but I was determined to hold my ground. I was just about to reiterate my refusal to discuss the case when an arm reached around me from behind and the delicate scent of lilacs informed me that someone very special was making her presence known. I turned to see the big blue eyes of Mary Alice smiling at me, and I felt a comforting sense of warmth flood through my body. Her tender touch never failed to excite me, and the broad smile on my face reflected the happiness she brought me.

She was just about the prettiest woman I've ever met, and I'd met some great looking ones over the years. She was small and trim and had all the right curves in all the right places. Her auburn hair was done up in a ponytail, as it usually was when she worked, and it made her seem even younger than her actual age of 35, which she shared with me only grudgingly.

She snuggled up next to me which made me proud and embarrassed at the same time. "I'm ready if you are," she said brightly.

For someone who had just spent the last eight hours on her feet lugging around trays of food and dirty dishes, she seemed lively and energetic; and I wondered how she could look so fresh and spirited.

"What's your hurry?" I asked. "I was just getting set to have a fresh cup of coffee and tell Sherman here all about our big chase last night."

She knew that I was just teasing Sherman and poked me in the ribs with her elbow as punishment. I groaned in mock pain, and she said, "I'm leaving with or without you, but I can offer you something better than Sherman's warmed-over coffee."

I raised my eyebrows and glanced at Sherman, who remained motionless at the counter, still hoping to hear something ... anything about the cattle thieves. But Mary Alice and I had better things in mind, so I said goodbye to Sherman and headed for the door with Mary Alice in tow.

"Do you mind if we go to your place tonight, Clint?" she asked. "I was called in early and my place is a total disaster."

Knowing Mary Alice, her place as a "total disaster" was better than mine on its best day; but if it suited her, it was fine with me.

"Sure," I replied, "No problem. I cleaned my place just a week or so ago and it's good for another few weeks."

She knew I was joking, but gave me a sour look and said something not worthy of a lady of her stature.

We both laughed as we walked arm-in-arm to my car. The autumn air was crisp and invigorating. In the west, the sun was making its descent, sending its golden rays spilling over the lofty mountain peaks. The view was spectacular and made everything seem right with the world. All of my cares seemed to disappear with Mary Alice at my side.

We arrived at my apartment and went inside. I was prepared to fix dinner, but I sensed that she was troubled about something, so we sat down together and I asked her what was going on.

"Oh, nothing, really," she said leaning in to me, and I gathered her in my arms, feeling her body mold itself into mine, as if we two were one, and waited for her to tell me what was on her mind.

Finally, she said, "It's that new girl, Jennifer. I just don't think she's going to work out."

This surprised me. I'd met the young woman just once, but she seemed very capable. She was young, attractive, had a great smile and personality, and reminded me of a younger version of Mary Alice. It was the first time I'd heard Mary Alice voice her disapproval of Jennifer, and it caught me off guard.

She must have sensed my reaction. "Oh, she can do the job, no question about it. It's just her darn attitude that gets me."

"What do you mean?" I asked, genuinely interested. I could tell that Mary Alice was quite stressed on this point and it bothered me.

"She's been working there three days now, and she thinks she knows it all. When I try to explain something to her, she makes excuses for why it should be done differently, and then goes on doing it her own way."

I sensed there was a personality conflict between the two women, and I knew I had to be careful about what I said.

"So, what does Sherman have to say about this?" I asked.

"Oh, Sherman's totally blind to what's going on," she said disgustedly. "All Jennifer has to do is give him a wink, strut that cute figure in front of him, and she can do no wrong."

"Well, sweetheart," I said, "if she's not doing her job correctly, I'm sure Sherman will see the light – eventually – and it will be up to him to get her straightened out, one way or the other. I wouldn't count him out just yet."

She pulled closer to me and I gave her a tight hug, hoping to reinforce my confidence that things would eventually work out.

"Yes, I suppose so. I guess I should be glad I've only got one more shift to work with her. Then she'll be on mornings and she'll be Hilda's problem. That will be a real trip," she said with a laugh.

I decided dinner could wait. Instead, I went to the refrigerator and grabbed us both a cold beer. I sat down next to her and pulled her close to me and she responded with a kiss on my cheek. I was pretty sure there was something else on her mind and I thought I knew what it was. But I wasn't going to open up that box because I knew she'd get to it when she was ready. I didn't have long to wait.

She took a long swallow from the bottle and said, "I've been thinking about you all day."

"I'm glad to hear that," I replied. "It makes me feel like I'm wanted."

She looked up at me with those sensuous brown eyes.

"Of course you're wanted – and needed, you silly man," she said with mock indignation. Then she laid her head against my chest, and I knew that what she wanted more than anything was just to be held, and I was happy to do just that.

"I've been worried about that telephone call from Nelson Bradford," she said. "I don't know if you can call it women's intuition or a premonition or what? I just have this fear that your meeting with the governor will somehow change our lives. And I like our life the way it is right now."

I stifled an urge to laugh. I felt she was being unnecessarily worried about tomorrow's meeting, but I didn't want to act like her fears were unimportant, even though I didn't share her concern.

"You can rest assured, sweetheart, that whatever is on the governor's mind will have absolutely no effect on me, you, or our relationship." I gave her a kiss on her cheek to seal the deal. "And even if he made me an offer too good to refuse, I would turn it down in a second if I thought it could come between us!"

I was absolutely confident that I meant what I said, but I wasn't sure she was convinced; and it bothered me that I wasn't able to allay her doubts. Of course, at that moment, I had no idea what the next twenty-four hours held for me.

"In case you might not have noticed," I said, "I'm pretty darned happy about the way things have worked out between us, and I'm not about to let anything or anyone change that."

She pulled away from me and there were tears in her eyes. "Promise?"

"Promise. Scout's honor," I replied and kissed her gently on her lips, and then on the tip of her nose.

Despite my best efforts to reassure Mary Alice, a lingering doubt raced through my mind because Mary Alice's women's intuition had been spot-on right before.

CHAPTER 4

Cooper's Landing was what's left of a small airfield that was used briefly during World War II as a training facility for local Air Force Reserve pilots. Between 1942 and 1943, Master's Field, as it was then known, was a regular beehive of activity, and Climax derived the benefit of the reserve officer's weekend binges in search of wine, women and song. After the war, the field fell into disrepair and eventually the U. S. government auctioned off the 144 acres of land that comprised the field to Hiram Johnson, a local businessman who had hopes of turning the field into a commercial airport for both private corporations and commercial airlines. He scraped up enough money to convert the administration building into a combination restaurant, lounge and coffee shop. There was some talk of getting one or two small commuter flights a day into Climax, but that never panned out.

Some of the maintenance buildings were converted into self-serve storage units and small warehouses. But the only real commercial activity remaining at the field was Kelly's Lounge, a hangout for a few ranchers and wranglers who, for one reason or another, prefer not to do their drinking in town.

Kelly – I wasn't sure if it was his first or last name – was a man of slender build and small stature who reminded me of a Leprechaun. He stood no more than five feet tall; probably weighed in at less than one hundred pounds, and might have had a successful career as a jockey. He had one of those faces that made it almost impossible to discern his age. There was not a single wrinkle or line in his face, which always bore a wide smile. His eyes virtually twinkled, and his voice rose and fell in melodic rhythm as he spoke.

I arrived at the airfield fifteen minutes early and entered Kelly's. The dulcet tones of Doris Day drifted from hidden speakers; a couple of men were hunched over the bar. Kelly greeted me warmly from behind the bar and pushed a cup of coffee my way.

"Just brewed it a couple minutes ago," he said. "Have a cup on me."

I thanked him and placed a couple of singles on the counter which he ignored.

"Don't get much traffic out here this time of the day, Sheriff," Kelly said in a jovial tone. "I hope this is not an official visit. I'm pretty sure I paid that parking ticket."

I laughed and held up my hands to reassure him that I wasn't there for that reason. "Just passing through, Kelly. I'm supposed to be picked up here at ten o 'clock."

I didn't want to discuss the details of my trip, but soon realized that I didn't need to. Kelly's eyes grew wide and his eyebrows hiked an inch or so farther up his forehead. "You waitin' for the governor's plane, Sheriff? It's the only one due here this afternoon, I hear. Big business up in Capitol City, I bet!"

"Just routine government work, Kelly," I said, sipping the strong brew. "I'll be back in time for dinner."

But Kelly was no fool, and he didn't buy my explanation. "Seems like he coulda just called you if all he wanted was to talk."

He had a valid point but I didn't comment and hoped he wouldn't press further.

Just as I finished the coffee, I heard the faint drone of an airplane engine somewhere in the distance. Kelly heard it too and craned his head to one side as if to direct his ear in the direction of the sound.

"King Air 350, sounds like. That'll be the governor's plane all right."

I thanked him for the coffee and followed him outside into the blazing sunlight. We watched as a sleek, twin propeller plane passed overhead, turned gracefully about a half mile out and approached the airstrip at a gentle angle, touching down just a hundred feet so from the edge of the landing strip. It taxied up to within fifty feet of where we stood and the pilot expertly brought the plane around and cut the engines.

Kelly walked up to the airplane, blocked the wheels and waited at the passenger door for someone inside to release the latch. The door swung open and a stairway folded neatly out. Almost immediately, Bradford Nelson appeared in the doorway and climbed nimbly down the stairs.

He was well over six feet tall and was built square and solid like a heavyweight boxer. I knew he was in his sixties, but the years had been good to him, and the best spas and medical care that money can buy probably had something to do with his rugged good looks. His tanned skin was the color of copper and his broad smile displayed perfect dentistry. His shaved head only enhanced the animal magnetism and power that radiated from him like the rays from the sun. He had steel-blue eyes that looked as if they could pierce right through you, an aquiline nose, and heavy dark eyebrows that could be considered menacing.

Bradford strode boldly down the ladder and headed for me without hesitation. He extended his right hand and grasped mine firmly but warmly. "Sheriff Harrison," he said, "it's good to see you."

With his reputation for being a man who possessed both power and charm and knowing how to use them to his own advantage, it was difficult for me to imagine anyone refusing him anything. This, I supposed, was why the governor had chosen him as his chief of staff.

I acknowledged his greeting and, while still holding my right hand in his, he stood before me with his left arm on my shoulder, peered into my face with those piercing blue eyes and said, "Sheriff, I must tell you that both the governor and I are real admirers of yours." His face was only a foot from mine as he spoke and his manner conveyed honesty and sincerity that was quite inviting. I could tell that he was accustomed to getting people to do his bidding, but in a way that made them happy to be doing it.

"We were very impressed with the way you wrapped up that mess with Tall Horse and his band of renegades," Bradford went on. "I hope you and I will have some time together when you can fill me in on all the details. It must be a fascinating story."

Before I could reply, we were walking toward the plane where he gestured for me to precede him up the stairs. I turned to Kelly who gave me a wave, and then I was in the plane with Nelson Bradford stepping in behind me.

The interior of the plane was compact but efficient and very handsomely appointed. Six deep leather chairs were arranged in club car fashion allowing for plenty of individual room and personal comfort; and could accommodate either business or pleasure. A small folding table was recessed into the wall and could be pulled out to facilitate paperwork or other work requiring a flat surface. In a small alcove there was a small desk equipped with a computer, 3-in-1 printer, and a couple of other electronic devices I didn't recognize. There was also a small galley equipped with sink, refrigerator and microwave oven. All the comforts of home and more, I thought to myself. The plane was not as luxurious as some used by members of the corporate elite, but it seemed like a very efficient way to get around the state, and no doubt served the needs of the governor quite well.

The door to the cockpit was open and I could see the pilot as he started the engines with a high-pitched whine. Nelson Bradford reached behind him, pushed a lever near the door and the stairway retreated back into the airplane hydraulically. He reached out, pulled the door toward the plane and secured it with a quick thrust of a lever.

Bradford gestured to one of the chairs and said, "Please sit down, Sheriff. We'll be airborne shortly."

I felt the plane move forward slowly, then pick up speed. A voice from the cockpit announced that he had been cleared for takeoff and asked us to please be seated and fasten our seat belts. I found mine pushed into the folds of the heavy leather chair, pulled it out and pushed the two ends together until they snapped with a comforting click. Bradford followed suit and we both sat back and listened as the pitch of the engines increased. In a few seconds the plane taxied to the end of the runway, made a sharp turn and then headed back down the runway with increasing speed. I was pushed back into the comfortable stuffing of the chair as the plane quickly accelerated, then lifted off.

Bradford gave me another one of those million-dollar grins and said, "She's quite a performer, isn't she?"

I decided to pop the question that had been on my mind since his telephone call the day before. "If you don't mind my asking, Mr. Bradford, I –"

"Please call me Nelson, Sheriff Harrison. May I call you Clint?" He beamed broadly at me.

"Nelson, then," I said, "I'm frankly a bit puzzled about why the governor has asked to meet with me. Is there anything that you ..."

He drew close to me and spoke in hushed tones, as if he were about to share a very important secret. "To tell you the truth, Clint, I really think that is something Governor Franklin needs to discuss with you personally. In the meantime, how about something to drink?"

He glanced at the gold Rolex on his left wrist. "We have about thirty-five minutes before we arrive in Capitol City and a good stiff drink always helps these flights go by a bit quicker for me."

I said a light beer would be fine and he gave me a reassuring smile.

"You'll find the bar here small but well-stocked. The governor has a preference for Coors Light, so you're in luck."

Without leaving his chair he reached forward and withdrew a cold bottle of beer from the small refrigerator and handed it to me. Turning the other way, he withdrew a quart of Canadian Club whiskey from a cabinet and poured several ounces into a glass, added three ice cubes from a cannister on a shelf, and extended the glass to me in a toast.

"To the governor," he said, and I returned the toast as our glasses clinked together. Meanwhile, a dozen unanswered questions raced through my mind.

"That was quite a story about those cattle thieves I read in the paper yesterday," Nelson said, flashing a bright smile. "What can you tell me about it?"

I looked out the window and marveled at the majestic snow-capped peaks of the Rocky Mountains directly beneath us.

"It was the result of good reconnaissance and a lot of hard work, topped off by a bit of luck," I replied, then spent the next 25 minutes reliving the details of our investigation, the chase, and its tragic aftermath. He listened with great interest and I could tell he loved a good action yarn.

"That's a hell of a tale, Clint." he said, his eyes sparkling with delight. "It's too damn bad about those rustlers, but you know, in a way, they got exactly what they deserved."

I shook my head sadly and said, "I'm not so sure, Nelson, but there are a lot of folks in my county who would agree with you."

"You know, Clint, I meant what I said earlier about how the governor and I feel about what you've done in the short time you've been in office. Jim Jenkins, God rest his soul, could not have found a better man to take over for him. We admire and respect courage and integrity, and it's clear that you have more than enough of both."

I didn't know where he was headed but I was humbled by his words and I thanked him.

"It's been interesting," I said, "that's for sure." Nelson laughed. "I'll bet it has."

Then he turned serious and said, "The governor is a good and decent man. He has a tough job and he needs help. I can't go into detail, but I can tell you that you are in a position to help him a lot more than you can imagine. I only hope you will listen to what he has to say with an open mind and consider all the ramifications before making your decision. And, whatever you do decide, we will respect your decision."

His words may have been meant to reassure me, but they had the opposite effect. Any uncertainty I had about my meeting with the governor had now been magnified tenfold and a sense of dread and foreboding came over me. But of course, it was too late to turn back now.

CHAPTER 5

We landed at the Capitol City Airport exactly forty minutes after taking off. We taxied to a restricted area and were met by a liveried driver in a black Lincoln Town Car and two uniformed State Troopers, who got into an unmarked state police car and quickly whisked us through a security gate at the rear of the airport. Within minutes, we were on the freeway heading west into the heart of Capitol City.

I'd seen pictures of the governor's mansion in the newspapers and on television, but I was not prepared for the stately elegance and serene majesty that greeted us as we drove through an electronically-controlled gate in the ten-foot high wrought-iron fence that served as a security perimeter. Dubbed "The Manor", the mansion had been built in the late nineteenth century by John Comstock, a wealthy oilman who bequeathed the estate to the state when he died in 1893. It's been the home of every governor since then, and has been expanded and renovated several times in the last century.

The thirty-acre estate sat atop a large hill that provided an awe-inspiring view of the Rushing River to the south. Large Doric columns highlighted a massive entrance that was served by a large U-shaped Ndriveway. The estate had its own botanical garden that was open to the public, and was supervised by state foresters. The Manor itself was huge and rambling and had a Georgian Neoclassical style. Servants' quarters and a five-car garage were on one side. Tennis courts and an outdoor pool could be seen through a grove of oak trees at the rear. I couldn't help wondering what the taxes would be on the place if it were still in private ownership, and I decided that it was definitely out of my price range. Nelson Bradford had been on his cell phone most of the time during the fifteen minutes it took us to drive to the Manor. That left me to enjoy the sights of the city, which I had visited only once before during a law enforcement conference two months earlier. Bradford finished his conversation just as we were being waved through the main gate by a uniformed officer.

"Sorry, Clint, but in this business, we have to stay connected," Bradford explained. "If we're not dealing with one crisis, we're trying to avoid another one before it gets started."

I suspected that he was a man who thrived on crisis the way some men thrived on sports. Turmoil and catastrophe are just part of his daily routine, I thought, happy that I didn't have the same lifestyle. He would be a good person to have on your side in a tough situation, and he could also be a very formidable opponent. I hoped I'd never have to find out just how daunting a foe he could be.

We got out of the car and I followed Bradford past a uniformed security guard and into an impressive foyer about half the size of an auditorium. I was intrigued by the elegance of some of the paintings hanging on the walls that resembled ones I'd once seen on display at the Metropolitan Museum of Art in New York City. Equally impressive were the sculptures and other works of art displayed on pedestals and in alcoves throughout the room. It looked more like a miniature art museum than someone's residence.

Bradford saw me eyeing the treasures and said, "Most of these pieces are on loan from various museums around the world. Very few of them actually belong to the state, and none of them belong to the governor."

Then he chuckled and said, "His own collection of art is much more modest than what you see here."

I followed Bradford through a series of offices, all occupied by men and women busy at their desks, working at a computer console, or engaged in animated telephone conversations.

We stopped abruptly before a secretary's desk occupied by a pert blonde woman who handed him a sheath of message slips and several file folders, and said, "The two on top need to be handled right away. The rest are only urgent."

Bradford accepted them without question; then the woman said, "I pulled the file on the Kramer appeal, and the consultant's report on the problems at Transportation. You'll need to review them before your four o'clock meeting with staff."

Bradford introduced me to Diane Jersey, his executive secretary. She impressed me as being highly efficient – someone who had just the right combination of organizational and administrative skills that a man like Bradford demanded. She was also dammed good looking.

Bradford turned to me. "Clint, I need to deal with a couple of these things right now, if you'll please excuse me." Then he addressed his secretary, "I imagine Clint is probably up for a good cup of coffee, Diane. He takes it black. Would you please see to it? Then let Mrs. Folsom know that Clint and I will be available to meet with the governor in about ten minutes."

He left, and I wondered how Bradford knew how I liked my coffee. Then I decided that there was probably quite a bit about me that he knew. He was just that kind of man.

Ms. Jersey rose and walked to an alcove at the rear of the room and returned a moment later carrying a large blue mug with the state seal embossed on it.

The aroma of fresh Columbian coffee was absolutely tantalizing. She smiled broadly, handed the mug to me, and I thanked her. She appeared to be in her early thirties, stood about five-feet-five in heels, and was well-proportioned. She was dressed demurely in a grey suit and white blouse. She wore her blonde hair pulled back and up off her shoulders. The effect was striking. She gestured for me to take a seat in one of the two chairs near her desk.

I had just finished the coffee when Nelson Bradford returned and said, "Governor Franklin will see us now."

I handed Ms. Jersey the coffee cup and rose to follow him down a long hallway. The governor's office was actually a series of several offices, most of which housed a frenetic clutter of assistants, secretaries and clerks busily engaged in an assortment of administrative duties.

We came at last to another office where I was introduced to Agnes Folsom, the governor's executive secretary. She was a matronly woman in her fifties who carried herself with grace and dignity, yet she was quite business-like in demeanor. She smiled a greeting and I followed Bradford into the governor's private office, which was very large and handsomely appointed.

One entire wall was dominated by a huge fireplace that reminded me of something from a mediaeval castle. The fire pit was a good six feet in height and at least ten feet wide. I could imagine an entire steer being roasted on a spit over a roaring fire.

A large ornate desk dominated the room, and was covered by an assortment of file folders, books and papers. I observed two telephones on the desk – one red and one white – and I wondered about the significance of their respective colors. A combination fax machine and printer, as well as three computer consoles and keyboards, and a small television were located on a table behind the governor's desk. A busy setup for a busy man, I thought.

A large floor-to-ceiling picture window ran the entire length of one wall, offering a majestic view of the river below, a large portion of the estate, and Capitol City in the distance. I was captivated by the spectacular beauty of the entire scene.

Governor Franklin was on the red phone when we entered. He waved us to two large leather chairs facing him and continued his conversation while we waited. I had met him briefly once before, when I attended a state law enforcement agency conference where he was the guest speaker. He was considered a political moderate, but had always been a strong supporter of local law enforcement, which I appreciated.

He finished his call and rose to greet us, giving me a chance to study him more carefully. He was tall – perhaps six-feet-four or five – and slender. He stood quite erect and was an imposing figure in both height and bearing.

He was impeccably attired in grey suit pants, a starched white shirt and a simple maroon tie. He wore French cuffs with gold cuff links bearing the seal of the state, which I later learned he gave out as gifts to state visitors. His red suspenders were a trademark that he'd worn for as long as anyone could remember.

His thinning hair was a brown-grey mix and he wore it straight back, giving him a somewhat severe look. His complexion was neutral and I guessed that he didn't spend a lot of time outdoors, or in a tanning salon, although I knew that he enjoyed an occasional round of golf. He had small hands and his nails were carefully manicured.

He reached across the desk and extended his hand to me, offering a firm handshake. He had a natural smile and a captivating twinkle in his brown eyes. Wire-rimmed glasses perched on the end of his nose reminded me of a merry elf. "Sheriff Harrison, it's a pleasure to see you. Please sit over here where we can be more comfortable."

We walked to an overstuffed couch near the fireplace; and he motioned Bradford and me to be seated. I did so, and Nelson Bradford sat down beside me.

Governor Franklin sat in a wing back chair facing us, reached for a coffee service next to him, and poured three cups of coffee, then handed one to Bradford and another to me. I thanked him and he said, "Sheriff Harrison, may I call you Clint?"

I nodded. He took a sip of his coffee, then said, "Clint, I know that you must be just a bit curious about why I asked you to come here today, and I apologize for any inconvenience this trip may have caused you."

I started to reply, but he held up a hand to cut me off. "Please believe me when I say that I would not have asked you to come here on such short notice if it were not a matter of some urgency."

I said nothing, and tried to control the tension that mounted inside me. It was clearly the governor's show, and I was anxious to know the purpose for the meeting, but I understood that he'd explain in due time.

The governor paused for a moment, looked out the window, and seemed to be lost in thought. Finally, he turned to me and said in a subdued voice, "What I am about to tell you, Clint, has to remain within this room. Whether you decide to help us or not – and I stress that this is your decision and your decision alone – what we speak of here and now must go no further."

His words sent a chill down my spine, and the sense of anxiety I'd experienced previously returned in spades. I remained in rapt attention and waited for the governor to continue.

"Clint, I know you're relatively new to this state. That's one of the reasons that Nelson suggested you for this assignment. Nevertheless, you've been around long enough that I assume you have a fair sense of the political landscape here in Colorado."

He looked at me quizzically, waiting for my reaction.

I had little interest in politics, but I knew enough to give him a shorthand version. "Yes, well ... I know that you are a Democrat elected two years ago by a substantial majority in a state that votes heavily Republican. And that your attack on political corruption was a major theme of your campaign."

The governor nodded, and I continued.

"You continue to enjoy a great deal of popular support, despite substantial opposition in the state legislature, which continues to be dominated by long-term Republicans and a few Independents who want nothing more than to preserve the status quo, and who resist any change that might threaten their own power base."

Governor Franklin smiled warmly. "You've managed to omit a few important details, Clint, but you're essentially correct. We've won some solid victories, and I'm hopeful that my popular support will continue long enough to earn me a second term in office, so I can continue the important work we've begun."

He paused long enough to drain the rest of his coffee and I followed suit. He offered me a refill but I declined, already feeling an unwelcome pressure on my kidneys.

The governor looked to Nelson, who said, "One of the keys to our political success has been the support of key Independents and a few Republicans who aren't afraid to break party ranks for the right reasons. None of these have been more important to us than Tom Powers."

Powers, I knew, was the extremely popular mayor of Capitol City. He was in his late forties, wealthy, politically solid, intelligent, articulate and black, all of which made for a formidable combination.

"Even though we represent different political parties," the governor continued, "Tom Powers and I work well together, and it's no secret that we need each other. I have pushed several of his pet projects through the legislature, and he has supported my political agenda on many key issues. Privately, I fully expect him to succeed me when my second term – assuming I get one – is completed."

Nelson Bradford cut in, "Powers has done an outstanding job of running this city in the last six years, and there's no one we would rather have as mayor of the largest city in the state."

I wasn't particularly interested in a history lesson on the local political scene and wondered where all this was headed, but I didn't have to wait long to find out.

Bradford continued, "What we're leading up to, Clint, is that Tom Powers has a very big problem that he is unable to deal with, and we've agreed to help him. Unfortunately, our involvement in this entire matter must be kept totally secret. Otherwise, it would look like we had no confidence in Powers, and that wouldn't be good for either of us."

He crossed his legs, picked a small piece of lint off his trousers, and went on, "Tom Powers came to me one week ago and told me that he had a situation that was so sensitive and so serious that he needed my help in solving it."

Both my interest and curiosity were at their peak, and I waited anxiously to hear "the rest of the story."

The governor lowered his voice an octave and said, "At first, we weren't sure how we could help him, but then Nelson came up with an idea and suggested I contact you."

He turned to Bradford who smiled, but said nothing.

"Nelson is quite a fan of yours, and this was not the first time your name had come up during our conversations."

This was high praise coming from Bradford, and I said, "That's very kind of you. I hope your expectations are justified."

"I don't think there's much doubt about that, Clint," the governor said emphatically. "We checked you out pretty thoroughly, and you match up to what we're looking for on every level. The only real question is whether you are willing to take on a very difficult and challenging assignment that must be handled with extreme sensitivity."

My curiosity was at full throttle now. "Well, Governor Franklin, I guess we won't know the answer to your question until I learn exactly what you need me for."

The governor leaned forward and put his hand on my arm with a reassuring grip. "That's all I can ask of you, Clint. Nothing more, nothing less."

I sat back and waited to hear his pitch. But nothing could have prepared me for what I was about to learn.

CHAPTER 6

The governor abruptly stood, clasped his hands behind his back and looked at me gravely. "You probably know, Clint, better than most people, that a well-run and efficient police department is essential in any large city. A poorly-run police department is – or can be – one of the biggest nightmares of any mayor."

I nodded. I'd seen numerous examples of what can happen in a police department with poor leadership. I was fortunate to have worked in a professional police agency run by a competent administrator; but I was aware of others that seemed continually mired in controversy and public criticism. I knew of officers in those departments who were victims of either political interference or mismanagement, or both. They eventually became spoiled by the system itself. It was an unfortunate situation, and I was blessed to have avoided such an experience.

"Mayor Powers has shared something that shocked me, and caught me totally off guard," the governor said sadly. "It appears that he has accidentally stumbled upon evidence of corruption at the highest levels in the department."

This came as a total surprise to me. The Capitol City Police Department was generally regarded as one of the finest of its size in the country; and it was certainly looked upon as the most professional in the state. Only a year ago the department had received its certificate of achievement from the Commission on Accreditation for Law Enforcement Agencies, which is a nationally-recognized body that is intended to achieve higher standards of conduct and performance for law enforcement agencies. CCPD was the first large department in the entire state to achieve this distinction, certifying that its policies, procedures, rules and regulations had been scrupulously examined by a panel of independent evaluators, and had been found to be consistent with nationally-endorsed standards. It was no small achievement, since there were less than five hundred police departments in the United States that had achieved this status. which required between two and four years of intensive and costly effort to achieve. Unfortunately, some municipalities saw little or no value in this, and refused to support this effort financially. To his credit, the Capitol City Chief of Police was able to mount a persuasive argument to Mayor Powers and the City Council that led them to provide the financial support to pursue this worthwhile goal.

As if reading the incredulity in my eyes, Governor Franklin said grimly, "I know what you're probably thinking, Clint. I had trouble believing it myself. But Mayor Powers provided me with convincing evidence to support his allegations."

"May I ask what kind of evidence?" I inquired.

Governor Franklin gestured to Bradford. Nelson rose and walked to a console next to the governor's desk. He opened the it to reveal a large-screen television. He pointed a remote control and punched a button.

The screen came to life, illuminating a blue background. Bradford punched another button and a few seconds later dark, shadowy images appeared.

We were watching a meeting between two men. They were in what appeared to be a small storeroom of some kind, with boxes, crates and cases of all sizes and descriptions piled high along one wall. The two men were seated at a small table on two wooden chairs facing each other. The room was dimly lit by a single light bulb that hung from the ceiling.

The scene had apparently been recorded by a hidden surveillance camera. Despite the poor lighting in the room, the black and white images on the screen were of reasonably good quality. But the audio was a different story. The voices faded in and out, making the conversation hard to understand.

One of the men appeared to be short and heavyset with broad shoulders and almost no neck. He wore a wide-brim hat that was tilted back on his head. He had dark eyebrows and long bushy sideburns that extended to the line of his jaw. He wore a light-colored sport coat, dark shirt and white tie and dark-colored trousers. His round face was dominated by a large, bulbous nose that looked as if it might have been broken once or twice and never properly reset.

The second man looked to be tall and well-built. He wore no hat and had a receding hairline. His face was long and angular, with deep-set eyes that, even in the poor lighting, seemed to glisten as he spoke. His dark hair was long and combed back on the sides. He wore a dark suit and white shirt complimented by a dark tie. He had the demeanor of a man who was used to having his own way, and relied on others to do his bidding.

Big Nose spoke with a deep, grave voice and I could only pick up snippets of what was said. "Your boys ... our people last night. The boss ... worried ... the shipment."

Glistening Eyes spoke with quiet authority. "He was ... stolen car ... weapon. The ... no choice."

Big Nose seemed unhappy with the reply and responded menacingly, "The boss ... big money! ... better not ... again ..."

Glistening Eyes did not seem to be at all intimidated by B. N. He replied, "Don't worry, the ... go away ... Tell him ... under control ... we keep ... bargain."

B. N. shook his head angrily. "What about the ... task force ... sniffing around? They are ... too close ... You need to ... before ..."

This time it was the G. Es' turn to shake his head. "These things ... go away. We have ... under control ... keep their investigators ... months."

B. N. paused to think about what he'd been told, shrugged his shoulders, then withdrew a thick manilla envelope from his jacket and handed it to G. E. "The boss ... happy ... taking care ... business."

Glistening Eyes accepted the envelope, opened it, and withdrew a stack of currency. He examined it carefully, then placed it back inside the envelope and stuck the envelope into the pocket of his suit coat. "... aim to please.'"

Both men stood and shook hands, turned, then disappeared off camera. The image faded abruptly and the screen returned to its original blue color.

The governor sat down and said, "I probably don't need to tell you what you've just seen."

I replied, "That appeared to be some kind of payoff, but I'm not sure who the parties are."

Nelson Bradford offered grimly, "Would it surprise you to know that the man accepting the cash was a ranking member of the Capitol City Police Department?"

That was a startling revelation if it was true. "How did you come to possess the video?"

The governor shook his head. "All I know is that it came in the mail addressed to Mayor Powers, who then turned it over to me. There was no return address, no note, nothing. We don't even know if the video is genuine. But if it is,

Mayor Powers has a very serious problem on his hands."

I still wasn't clear on this point. "Are you suggesting this has something to do with the Capitol City Police Department?"

Bradford interjected, "There's no question about that, Clint. We are certain that the man accepting the envelope is Captain Lawrence Wilkins, head of the Criminal Investigation Division of the CCPD. The other man has been identified as Frank (Frankie) DeSalvo, the underboss of the organized crime syndicate in this area."

Now I understood Mayor Power's dilemma, but I still didn't see what this had to do with me.

As if reading my thoughts, Governor Franklin said, "I believe what you've just seen, Clint, is clear evidence of corruption at the highest level of the Capitol City Police Department."

Nelson Bradford abruptly stood and extended his arm to me. "You see, Clint, Captain Lawrence Wilkins is one of the most trusted and respected members of the CCPD. He's considered to be Chief Ryan's right-hand man and the person in whom the Chief places great trust. He's also likely to succeed Chief Ryan when the chief retires in two years. If Wilkins is dirty, it can only mean that the corruption extends to the Chief of Police as well."

It occurred to me that both Governor Franklin and Nelson Bradford might be way off base in their assumptions. "First of all, Governor, you don't know if the video you've just shown me is authentic or not. It could have been doctored to set this fellow Wilkins up. A person that high up in the granulation must have a few enemies willing to do whatever they can to take him down."

Without waiting for a response, I continued, "Second, even if this Captain

Wilkins is engaged in illegal activity, it does not necessarily follow that Chief Ryan is involved. I know of many cases that will prove this point only too well."

To drive the point home, I said, "Even if you believe that Captain Wilkins is involved in bribery, you should be talking to the local District Attorney, or even to the state's Attorney General. They have concurrent jurisdiction over such matters and have trained agents capable of conducting an investigation that will reveal the full extent of the corruption within the department. You certainly don't need to involve someone like me."

The governor shook his head, but before he could speak, Bradford interjected, "There are a couple of things you should know, Clint, that may help you understand why we've come to you. First, the State's Attorney in Capitol City is David Duncan, who is a reasonably good man and not a bad prosecutor. But his sister, Annabelle, is married to Patricia Ryan, who happens to be the daughter of Chief Jack Ryan. It would be a very frigid day in Hades before Dave Duncan would seek an indictment against his own father-in-law or, for that matter, one of Chief Ryan's most trusted people."

I was beginning to see his point, but there was still one other option, or so I thought. "Well, then," I said, "that still leaves the state's Attorney General."

Governor Franklin made a face as if he had just eaten a sour apple. "Ah, yes, and now we come to our illustrious Attorney General of the state, Ms. Grace Blackburn, who would single-handedly dismantle City Hall, brick by brick, if she thought it would help her build her own political power base."

I remembered seeing Ms. Blackburn on television recently. She was announcing the unveiling of a new organized crime task force that she'd managed to put together with several hundred thousand dollars from the U. S. Department of Justice. She was an attractive woman who seemed poised, articulate and intelligent.

The governor obviously didn't have a very favorable impression of the state's Attorney General, however, and Nelson Bradford explained, "Grace Blackburn is probably one of the most vindictive, vengeful, manipulative, politically ambitious and spiteful women I've ever had the displeasure of meeting."

I was stunned at Bradford's words. It certainly wasn't the impression I had of Ms. Blackburn, and I wondered why he felt so strongly about her. I didn't have to wait long to find out.

Governor Franklin leaned forward in his seat. "Grace Blackburn will stop at nothing to get what she wants. And what she wants right now is to be governor."

Bradford cut in, "And we feel very strongly that Grace Blackburn as governor would be one of the worst things that could happen to this state."

This was news to me. Even though I occupied an elective position, I'd never run for office and considered myself politically neutral. Nevertheless, I knew that politics could sometimes be a dirty business, so nothing he said surprised me.

Bradford continued, "Grace is being bankrolled by some of her right-wing friends in Washington who are the same people who've provided the funding for her organized crime task force. While that task force appeals to many people, and has a lot of support among law enforcement personnel, its real purpose is to dig up dirt on politicians and public officials in order to gain popular support for her. To the general public, she is waging a one-women war on vice and corruption. But to the political insiders, her ambitions to go much higher than the governor's office."

Being a newcomer in the political arena, I was a bit naive about the high stakes infighting that goes on at the state and national level, and didn't really care much about it. While I could appreciate the governor's dislike for Grace Blackburn political tactics and ambition, I still wasn't sure why he was so opposed having her office conduct the investigation.

As if reading my mind, Bradford explained. "You see, Clint, we have very reliable information that one of Grace Blackburn's top priorities is to place the CCPD under the authority of her office."

"That's pretty far-fetched," I responded. "How could something like that ever happen?"

Governor Franklin replied, "Unfortunately, Clint, Ms. Blackburn plans to use an obscure provision in our state constitution. It provides for the office of the state's attorney general to extend authority over any local agency of government in the state. This could be done under circumstances in which it can be clearly demonstrated that local control and management is unable to assure that the agency is responsive to the welfare of the people served by that agency."

"That's incredible," I said. "Has that provision ever been invoked?" "Actually, it has," Bradford said ruefully, "and with disastrous results."

"Like what?"

Bradford said, "Way back in 1901, the politics in this state got a little crazy – even crazier than they are today – and a fellow by the name of Hiram Goldfarb, whose claim to fame was that he owned and operated a series of bawdy houses here in Capitol City, got himself elected as the state's attorney general. Fortunately for the people of the state, he served less than one full term, but during that time, his office was up for sale to the highest bidder."

"It was one of the saddest periods of our state's otherwise glorious history," Franklin observed.

Bradford continued, "It was that, all right. Under Hiram's administration the place was wide open and corruption was rampant. And one of his most notorious moves was to manufacture claims of dishonesty and mismanagement by the Wells County Commissioners."

"Why would he do that?" I asked.

Governor Franklin explained, "Because in those days, Wells County was the site of one of the richest gold mining operations in the state, and the county commissioners had exclusive jurisdiction in awarding certificates of operation to the mine operators."

Bradford went on, "Goldfarb saw an opportunity to make some easy money because the mines there were reported to be worth tens of millions of dollars. So, he used this same 'obscure' statute to take over control of county government by manufacturing false claims of corruption and mismanagement by the county commissioners. This gave him the opportunity to install his own commissioners, and charge exorbitant fees to the mine owners for their certificates of operation."

I shook my head. "How could he get away with such a thing?" "He didn't – not for long, at least," Bradford replied cheerfully.

"When the corruption in Goldfarb's office became so blatant," Governor Franklin said, "the people of the state rose up in protest and eventually succeeded in getting him recalled before his term of office was over."

"Sounds like he should've gone to prison," I observed.

"He should have, and nearly did," Bradford said. "He and several members of his administration were prosecuted and convicted on a variety of charges. Several of them drew long prison terms, but Goldfarb died before he could be sentenced."

"That's an amazing story," I said, shaking my head. "Why didn't they get the law changed after all that?"

"Some legislators made a half-heated effort to," Governor Franklin said, "but there was just not enough support for it and the whole thing eventually just died off and was forgotten."

"Until now," Bradford observed.

"So, you really think there's a chance Grace Blackburn might try the same thing with the police department here in Capitol City?"

"There's no doubt about it," Governor Franklin said gravely.

"Let's just say we have it from a very reliable source," Bradford confirmed.

Governor Franklin made a hard face. "If there is corruption in the CCPD – and we pray there is not – it's essential that it be uncovered by an independent third-party such as yourself, rather than Grace Blackburn. There is no question that if her people conduct an investigation and end up finding corruption in the police department, we could be right back where we were one hundred and twenty years ago."

Bradford added, "And we just cannot stand by and let that happen." "So, Clint, you must understand the dilemma we find ourselves in," the Governor said resolutely.

"I can certainly understand the predicament you have on your hands" I concurred. "It seems that the person who can help you deal with this situation is the worst possible person to turn to."

"Which is exactly why we need your help," the governor said emphatically. "We need someone to look into this who has no hidden agenda, and who can expose the corruption – if there is any – before the state's Attorney General can use the information to her own advantage. If we can root out the evil in the CCPD ourselves, it will not only solidify our own political support, it will take a lot of the air out of her political balloon."

But I still wasn't sure exactly what they had in mind. "Just how do I figure into your plans, Governor? I have no official standing in this county, and I have very few contacts in the state outside my own county. Besides, I have my own job to do as sheriff."

Bradford had anticipated my question. "We think we have the perfect angle to get you set up in the police department in a position where you will have access to everything you need. And we can open all the doors you'll need opened. As you may know, Clint, the CCPD has been the beneficiary of a number of sizable grants from the state and federal government over the last several years. In fact, Chief Ryan has managed to take in well in excess of twelve million dollars in state and federal grants that have been used to purchase everything from in-car cameras and laptop computers, to voice stress analyzers, to one of the most sophisticated management information systems of any police department in the country."

He was right. It was generally known that the CCPD was a very technologically-advanced law enforcement agency, and much of that was due to the influx of state and federal dollars. It was no secret that Chief Ryan had done an admirable job of attracting grant money to help supplement his own city budget.

Governor Franklin spoke up, "You see, Clint, there is a provision in the law providing that, for certain of these grants, there must be an independent audit completed to ensure that the grant monies are being used in the manner provided by law, and for the purpose stated in the grant award. The language calling for these audits is rather vague, which permits a great deal of latitude in how these audits are to be conducted."

Bradford explained, "Such audits may be conducted by either the state or federal government, or by an independent contractor. As a matter of principle, such audits are often waived by the government, providing certain certifications are performed by the grantee agency."

I was beginning to see where he was going and I had to admit that it was a perfect cover for an internal investigation of the CCPD. But it seemed to me that getting access to the necessary files and information could be difficult. No one in the police department – especially Chief Ryan or Captain Wilkins – could be expected to voluntarily submit incriminating information to an outsider, even if the stated purpose of the probe was legitimate.

"I have to admit that your plan has some merit," I said, "but I still don't believe that I am the right person for the job. Besides, you will need to have a team of two or three people running such an investigation. There's no way that one person can accomplish what you need to have done."

Bradford smiled broadly. I should have known that he had already worked out all the details.

"We're convinced that you are the perfect choice for the assignment, Clint. You have the perfect background. You know your way inside a police agency, you've been a prosecutor and know how to build a case. You can talk to cops. And you know how to gather evidence. Your intelligence, honesty and courage are undeniable."

Governor Franklin said earnestly, "Frankly, Clint, we don't know of anyone else who can do the job if you turn us down."

The governor's words hit home with me, and I felt my resistance weakening. I could see the sincerity in his eyes and it made me want to agree to help him, but I wasn't totally convinced that I was right for the job he needed done.

"And we agree," Bradford said, "that this cannot be a one-man operation. We have two highly-skilled investigators from the state's Criminal Investigation Division, Office of Special Operations, available to work with you strictly on an undercover basis. They will be yours for the duration of the operation."

"But this investigation may take a considerable amount of time," I said. "I still have my own job to do. I can't simply walk away and leave the sheriff's department without –"

Once again, Bradford had anticipated my objection. "You have a very capable Chief Deputy in Bruce Johnson. We've checked him out, and we believe he'll be able to run things in El Dorado County during your absence. At any rate, we don't expect that you'll be gone from your post all that long – a month at most."

Bradford had obviously given this a lot of thought and seemed to have an answer for every objection I could come up with. Despite my misgivings, the offer was tempting.

The governor stepped in to make his own pitch. "Clint, I realize this is short notice, but we need to have this investigation completed in thirty days. We are convinced that Grace Blackburn may already be sniffing around, and may have stumbled onto some of the same information we have. If this is the case, we need to move fast. Thirty days is the absolute deadline for completing the assignment, and we hope that it can be wrapped up even sooner."

They were asking a lot of me, and I wanted more time to think over their proposal, but I knew the governor expected an answer. Despite my reservations, I had to admit that it was a challenging offer. If there was corruption in the police department, someone needed to expose it. If there was not, that needed to be known as well. Someone with no debt to settle – no ulterior motive – needed to take on this assignment.

"Well, Clint," Bradford said, "you've heard the situation as we know it. Now all we need to know is ... how soon you can start?"

Bradford clearly was a man accustomed to having his own way. He and the governor stared at me expectantly, and I knew there was no way I could stall them.

"I guess I'm your man, then. I'll do the best I can.

Governor Franklin's eyes brightened and he smiled broadly while Bradford reached out and patted me on the back, saying, "Great to have you on board, Clint. You've just taken a hellava load off our shoulders."

"We're prepared to offer you a significant honorarium for your services, Clint," Bradford said.

I shook his hand. "That's not necessary. I receive an adequate salary in Climax. I'm more than happy to help out without additional compensation."

"That's very decent of you, Clint," Governor Franklin said, "but we will certainly cover your lodging and all expenses while you're in town."

"That will be fine," I replied, "but before I go, Governor, I'd like to have the original video to take with me."

Bradford started to object, but the governor cut him off. "Why do you need the original rather than a copy, may I ask?"

"I need to have it checked out."

Bradford gave me a dubious look. "By whom? We have some very good forensic scientists in our –"

I cut him off abruptly. "Governor, as of now, you need to keep this investigation at arm's length. I have a contact at the FBI lab in Quantico who can be trusted to keep my inquiry absolutely confidential. I'd like to ask him to take a look at the video."

Despite Bradford's uncertainty, the governor said, "I see your point, Clint. From here on, it's your case, and you must do what you think best."

The governor motioned to Bradford, who went to the console, withdrew a small thumb drive and handed it to me. I pocketed it and promised, "I'll have it checked out as soon as possible. It's the only evidence we had at this point, and it's essential that I have it evaluated to ensure that it is genuine."

* * *

On the flight back to Climax, Bradford filled me in on the details I'd need as I began my investigation. I agreed to return to Capitol City the following Monday – in just four short days.

"You'll be contacted by our two undercover operatives as soon as you arrive in town," Bradford concluded. Then he withdrew a package from his briefcase and handed me three small cell phones. "You'll need to communicate with the members of your team while you're in Capitol City," he said. "These are the new Dataphone X Series. They've been specially modified for undercover assignments such as this. They are protected against jamming and eavesdropping, and are pre-programmed with an automatic speed dial for quicker communication between you and your team."

They looked like ordinary cell phones, but it turned out they were quite different than any I'd used before.

Bradford explained, "These phones have GPS tracking capability so that you will know where each of you are at all times, even if you're unable to communicate, and even if the unit is turned off."

He went on to explain a few additional features of the phones, and I could see that they'd certainly come in handy. This guy thinks of everything.

By the time we arrived back in Climax, it was nearly dinner time, and I was famished. I figured I could count on Mary Alice to prepare a great meal, and I knew she'd be anxious to know all about my meeting with the governor. Unfortunately, she wouldn't be prepared for what I had to tell her, and I knew she wouldn't be happy with the news. I was already beginning to wonder what I'd gotten myself into, and how I'd explain it to her.

CHAPTER 7

Carlos Ortega surveyed his surroundings with a mixture of repugnance and anticipation. The small, six-by-eight cell had been his home for the last nine months, and he was looking forward to leaving it for the last time. He'd slept very little last night, his mind churning with the details of what was about to unfold. In just an hour, he'd be on his way to freedom, and then he'd put a plan into play that had occupied his every waking moment since his arrest.

Carlos was a short, wiry, dark-skinned man whose body was tough and strong, the result of many years of hard labor in the lettuce fields of Bakersfield. As an enterprising teenager, he discovered a much easier way to earn money and help support his widowed mother and seven young siblings. A cousin introduced him to the easy money to be made by selling illicit drugs to those stupid enough to use them to ease the pain of their dreary lives.

Carlos had never used drugs of any kind, but he knew very well how easy it was to fall into the unforgiving, downward spiral of addiction. At the age of sixteen, Carlos had discovered one of his best friends dead with a needle in his arm, but this had done nothing to convince him to seek a less precarious means of making money. If anything, the sight of young Eduardo lying in the refuse-strewn alley with the needle still stuck in his arm, made Carlos even more resolved to defy the system that forced young men like him into a life of crime.

Now, nearly thirty years later, he was proud of what he'd achieved. In a very short time, he'd risen through the ranks from a petty street-level drug pusher to the top echelon of a major cartel that dominated the illegal drug trade in Southern California.

His rise had been marked by a great deal of violence, bloodshed, and several bodies along the way. But that was the price to be paid to get ahead in the illegal drug business. Ortega had no second thoughts about what he'd had to do to get where he wanted to be. He was prepared to do whatever it took, including cold-blooded murder, to achieve his goals.

If it hadn't been for the loose lips and drug-induced mind of one of his trusted lieutenants – who suffered the ultimate penalty for his carelessness and stupidly – Carlos would be relaxing on the warm, white sands of his estate near Cozumel rather than rotting here in the federal detention center in Los Angeles.

He certainly had no regrets about giving the order to kill Clint Harrison, the Assistant District Attorney in Los Angeles who had headed up the task force organized to take down his criminal empire. Harrison had been a thorn in his side since taking on that assignment and had continually made his life miserable. Ortega's only disappointment was that the car bomb meant for Harrison killed his wife and young son instead. Carlos felt no remorse whatsoever for killing two innocent people. He had long ago learned that he could only survive in the life he'd chosen by forgoing the emotions of guilt, empathy and compassion that made other men weak and ineffectual.

Actually, killing Harrison's wife and son gave him almost the same satisfaction as if Harrison himself had been killed by the blast. He'd struck back at Clint Harrison, and that was the important thing. But that wasn't enough. Harrison still must pay for the damage he'd done to Carlos' enterprise, and nothing short of Harrison's own death would be sufficient.

Even though the murders had taken its toll on Harrison – he'd quit his job and dropped out of sight – Carlos wasn't satisfied. Ortega's sources had managed to locate Harrison in a small town in a remote corner of Colorado where he'd been appointed sheriff. But that badge wouldn't keep Carlos from having his revenge.

Thanks to Harrison and his task force, Ortega had been arrested for drug trafficking and was scheduled to go to trial middle of next year. The skillful maneuvering of his $900-an-hour attorneys had managed to push back the trial date countless times, but his long period of isolation and deprivation was about to come to an abrupt end, and he could barely contain his excitement as his mind raced over the events that were about to unfold. A smile played on his lips as he joked to himself that he was doing the good people of Los Angeles a favor by saving them the expense of a long legal battle. Would they be thankful? No, probably not.

Daily jailhouse routine was the best thing Carlos had going for him, and he knew the procedure by heart. He was counting on his jailers' rigorous commitment to their regular, monotonous drill to make everything fall into place. They'd performed it countless times before –

thanks to the numerous delays and continuances arranged by his attorneys – and had never deviated from their long-established procedures by as much as a minute. At precisely 11:40 AM, the detention center guards arrived to escort him to the holding cell where he'd be searched for what seemed like the hundredth time, then placed in handcuffs and leg irons, just in time to be turned over to four U. S. Marshals, who'd escort him to the federal courthouse, less than a mile away.

At precisely ten minutes before noon, he was placed in the back of the prisoner van and locked into position, with the same two marshals sitting on a bench on either side of him; and two other marshals in the cab. Having made this trip many times before, he knew both men on a first-name basis, but they were not the friendly sort, and there was only a minimum of conversation between them. It was a monotonous routine for them, and Ortega's cooperative attitude may have prompted them to relax their vigilance just enough for his plan to succeed.

The driver's compartment was separated from the rear of the van by a metal screen and a bullet-resistant plastic shield. Solid steel benches, equipped with metal rings for attaching handcuffs and leg irons, provided the seating in the rear. Right on schedule, the prisoner van pulled out from the detention center and headed north on Alameda toward the federal courthouse. The ride normally took only four minutes in heavy traffic.

They would be met at the district court building by a phalanx of court guards who'd escort him and the two marshals into the federal lockup located in the basement of the courthouse. But this time would be different, as his scheduled arrival was not going to take place. He had arranged a very big surprise for all of them, and he couldn't wait to see their stunned faces when they realized that today, things were not going to go as they had planned.

Traffic on North Alameda was congested, as would be expected at high noon on a Monday, and that fit right into his plan, Ortega was sitting between the two stone-faced marshals as the van bumped and rattled toward its destination. When the transport vehicle suddenly braked, Carlos looked through the plastic barrier that separated the rear of the van from the driver's compartment. He saw a large furniture delivery truck double-parked, forcing two lanes of traffic to converge into a single lane. When they reached the delivery truck, a cargo van pulled up alongside the prisoner van and slowed, forcing it to a stop.

Before either of the two guards in the driver's compartment could react, four masked men jumped from the cargo van. Two of the masked men, carrying Barrett M82 automatic weapons, rushed to the cab of the prisoner van and fired at the windshield. The 50-caliber rounds were too powerful even for the bullet-resistant glass. The two marshals slumped in their seats, their heads and shoulders ripped apart by the savage fire from the automatic weapons.

While this was happening, the two other masked men went to the rear of the van and placed an explosive charge on a rear door, then ducked for cover.

The two marshals on either side of Ortega were unprepared for the thunderous explosion that rocked the van and blew one of the rear doors off its hinges, filling the rear of the van with dark, acrid smoke. Carlos, knowing what to expect, had shielded himself from the blast by maneuvering behind the marshal closest to the door. Both marshals were dazed and neither was able to react when one of the masked gunmen hopped into the rear of the van and fired a .22 caliber round at close range into the head of the marshal in front of Carlos, then at the second one, instantly killing both men.

Ortega was choking and coughing as the two men, now wearing gas masks, used bolt cutters to cut the handcuffs and leg irons from the bench and carry him out of the van, then help him through the open door of the delivery truck, which was already moving through heavy traffic as the rear door closed behind them.

Manuel, one of the two men in the rear of the van, removed his gas mask and said in Spanish, "You okay, Carlos?"

Manuel was short and stocky and had a youthful face, a large bushy mustache and thick black eyebrows.

Carlos stared back at him with coal-black eyes and said, "Yeah, Manuel, I'm okay. You guys did good."

Both men knew that was high praise coming from Ortega, who seldom paid anyone a compliment.

The second man, Hector, removed his gas mask and helped Carlos into a sitting position on one of the two benches, then took out a universal key and removed the cuffs from Ortega's wrists and then the leg irons.

Carlos rubbed his wrists where the cuffs had chaffed him.

Hector was tall and lean with a long, angular face and shaved head.

He said, "You're lookin' good, Carlos." Ortega ignored the statement.

Manual grinned and said, "Your plan worked just like you said it would."

Carlos sneered, "Lucky for you, huh?" In his world success was expected and failure was unforgivable.

They sat silently and held on to the bench as the truck bounced and veered crazily from side to side moving quickly through traffic, then shot up an on-ramp leading to the interstate highway.

The van sped toward its destination with Carlos deep in thought. The pain and frustration of being locked up like a caged animal was behind him now; but the suffering he'd experienced would not go away easily, and revenge was on his mind. There was important work to be done, and Carlos needed to spend some serious time contemplating about how to accomplish something he'd been thinking about since his first day behind bars.

Two hours later, after switching vehicles twice and cutting back over their route three times to make sure they weren't followed, Ortega and his rescuers pulled into a garage behind a small, one-story home in East Los Angeles. A tall hedgerow surrounded the house and offered perfect cover, safe from the prying eyes of nosey neighbors. Manuel and Hector exited quickly and escorted Ortega inside, while the two men in the front of the van drove off to dispose of the vehicle that had been stolen only hours earlier.

They passed through a small kitchen and Manuel led them into an adjoining living room. The place was modest but comfortable, and had been carefully selected as a safe house where Ortega and his crew could plan their next move.

Ortega was well aware that many of the houses he might ordinarily visit would probably be under surveillance by the drug task force that was still hunting members of his family enterprise. This place was far less opulent than what he was used to, but it was certainly an improvement over the six-by-eight cell he'd recently inhabited as a guest of the government.

Manuel went to the refrigerator and took out several bottles of cold Dos Equis beer and handed the first one to Ortega, then the others. It had been months since Carlos had tasted the savory brew and it was delicious.

The men drank and waited obediently for Carlos to say something.

Finally, he looked at Hector. "Where's the stuff?"

Hector jerked his thumb toward the bedroom. "In there." Carlos took a deep gulp of his beer, then rose to see for himself.

Manuel and Hector followed as Carlos went to a wooden crate marked in bold, red letters: "EXPLOSIVES"

He said to Hector, "Open it."

The lid of the box had already been pried loose, and Hector gently lifted it to display a dozen neatly-stacked packets of C4 explosive. Each one contained in a Mylar-film wrapper.

Ortega asked, "What did it cost me?"

Hector shrugged. "Not much. Our friends were willing to make a trade. This stuff for four kilos of uncut cocaine."

Ortega stared daggers at Hector. "You shoulda got it for three kilos."

Hector winced, but said nothing.

Ortega turned to Manuel. "You got anything new on Harrison?"

Manuel frowned. "Sorry, no. He's still out there in Colorado in that shithole town, Climax. You already know they made him sheriff after the old guy died."

Carlos said more to himself, "Yeah, but no lousy badge is gonna stop me."

The three men returned to the other room and sat down. Carlos looked at Hector and asked, "Where's Ramirez?"

Hector hesitated. "Don't know for sure, Carlos. You want me to get hold of him?"

Carlos gave Hector a deadly stare. "What do you think?"

Hector jumped up and retrieved his cell phone from his shirt pocket, consulted his directory, and dialed a number.

"Yeah?" the voice on the other end was icy and had the texture of broken glass.

Hector relayed Ortega's message, then disconnected. "He's on his way. Should be here sometime tonight."

Carlos greeted the news with silence, his mind continually in motion. Santiago Ramirez was a stone-cold killer who loved his work. Carlos had a job for him that would please both of them.

CHAPTER 8

Over the weekend, Mary Alice and I had plenty of time to talk about my new assignment. To say that she wasn't happy about the news was an understatement. In the year that we'd been together, I'd never seen her as unhappy as she was when I informed her what I'd taken on, and nothing I could say seemed to mollify her.

"Why didn't you just tell the governor you're too busy?" she demanded to know.

I'd asked myself the same thing on the way back from Capitol City, but couldn't come up with a good answer.

"You just don't tell the governor no when he asks you to do something as important as this," I said emphatically. Without letting her know the exact nature, I tried to explain just how important the assignment was, but my argument fell on deaf ears. She wasn't happy about my leaving, even when I promised to call her every day. Maybe for the first time, I realized just how attached to me she'd become. But I felt a deep obligation to get to the bottom of things in the CCPD. If there was corruption there – especially at the highest level – it needed to be exposed. I felt compelled by my sense of duty and honor to take on the challenge.

The following day I met with Bruce Johnson and briefed him on my new assignment. I trusted Bruce implicitly, but the sensitivity of the assignment compelled me to limit the number of people who knew the real purpose. He assured me he'd keep the matter under wraps and I knew I could count on him.

I assured Bruce that I could be reached by text, cell, or email if anything out of the ordinary came up – something I considered highly unlikely. The budget was done, the cattle thefts had been quelled, the remaining rustler was behind bars awaiting trial, and I expected things should be fairly quiet for the foreseeable future. Bruce, being something of a laid-back kind of guy, took my absence in stride and didn't seem to mind the added responsibility I'd placed on his shoulders. "No problem, boss, I gotcha covered," was his only response.

I called an old friend of mine, Herb Jenkins, one of the top men at the FBI's Forensic Sciences Unit in Quantico, Virginia. I got through to him right away and explained what I needed. He said to overnight the video to him and he'd get right on it and let me know whether it was authentic or had been altered in some way.

After making a copy for myself, I packaged up the thumb drive, addressed it to Herb Jenkins, and gave it to Bruce Johnson with instructions to overnight it to Herb. He accepted it without question and promised to take care of it first thing in the morning. With any luck, I'd hear something back from Herb within a week.

After a tearful goodbye with Mary Alice, I got packed and was on the road to Capitol City early Monday morning. The eight-hour drive took me through some of the most beautiful mountains in the continental United States. It was early summer, the temperature was in the mid-70s, the sky was sparkling blue, and I enjoyed the breathtaking vistas of the majestic, snow-covered peaks that towered above me.

As I drove, I made a mental checklist of things I needed to do when I arrived in Capitol City. My first priority was to contact the two undercover agents who'd be working with me. I was very curious about what they might have to offer, and how I could make the best use of their skills and experience.

I was jarred from my reverie by the ringing of my cell phone. I figured it was Mary Alice telling me that I'd forgotten to pack something, or reminding me to call her just as soon as I arrived. But when I looked at the screen, I saw that it was a call from the 310 area code: Los Angeles. I hadn't spoken with anyone from there in months and I didn't recognize the number.

"Hello?" I answered tentatively. "Clint?"

It was a man's voice, and vaguely familiar, but I couldn't put a name or face on it.

"Yes," I said, "this is Sheriff Harrison."

"Clint, this is Sam Warden from the U. S. Marshal's Office in L. A. We spoke a while back."

The recognition washed over me with a sense of dread. Warden had called me several months earlier to bring me up to date on the status of Carlos Ortega, who was about to be tried for arranging the murder of my wife and young son. Ortega's court date was still some weeks out, and I had a premonition that Warden's call was not going to make my day. "Yes, Sam. What is it?"

He hesitated for a moment, which heightened the tension I already felt, then said, "Well, Clint, It's about Ortega." The tone of his voice confirmed the dread I already felt.

"I figured that, Sam," I said. "What about him?"

He cleared his voice, hesitated again, then said, "He's out, Clint.

There's no other way to say it – he's back on the street."

The news hit me with the force of a pile driver. "What do you mean 'he's out,' Sam? How can that be? He's being held without bail. Did some high-priced lawyer get him released?"

Overwhelmed by frustration and anger, I was unable to think clearly. I pulled my car over to the shoulder of the road and sat there, too upset to concentrate on driving. My chest heaved and my pulse raced. I reached for the bottle of water in the console and drank heavily, trying to regain control of my emotions.

Finally, Sam said, "No, nothing like that, Clint."

He hesitated again, then said, "I wish I didn't have to tell you this, Clint, but Ortega escaped from custody earlier today. He was being transported to court when –"

I cut him off mid-sentence. "How in the hell did that happen, Sam? I thought he was under heavy guard!"

"Yeah, well, we thought so too," he said, and I sensed his own frustration at being the one to bring me the bad news.

"There was some kind of a security breakdown. I don't have all the facts. The four guards with him were all killed. It was all-around screw up, I can tell you that for sure."

I sat there trying to calm myself as he filled me in on the details as he knew them. The investigation was still unfolding – the break had occurred only a few hours earlier. By now they would have mounted a massive manhunt for Ortega, but he was cunning and a pathological killer, and there was no doubt in my mind that he'd be seeking revenge against me, just as he'd done two years earlier. The thought of that horrible day when my wife and son had been killed in a bomb blast meant for me sent chills down my spine. Was I facing that same threat again?

"Clint, we've got a task force of FBI, The U. S. Marshal's Office, DEA, Los Angeles City and County working on this. This city is shut down tight as a drum. It'll be tough for him to make a move without being picked up. Hopefully, he'll be back in our hands in less than 48 hours."

His words were intended to be reassuring, but I wasn't convinced.

Warden apologized again and promised to keep me updated on their progress then disconnected. I was absolutely sure that Ortega would manage to elude their search efforts. and I was equally certain that I'd not heard the last of Carlos Ortega, who had a sizable network of resources available to him. I needed to be prepared for any eventuality. Once again, I had second thoughts about taking on this assignment.

I resumed my drive and called Bruce Johnson to tell him about Ortega's escape, and warn him that one or more of his crew might be on the way to Climax looking for me. I gave him Sam Warden's cell number and suggested he call to get the particulars on any of Ortega's known associates, and to be kept in the loop on any updates.

"Consider it done, Clint, I'll get right on it," Bruce replied. "Anything else?"

I hesitated, then said, "Yes, Bruce. Please keep an eye on Mary Alice for me. This guy Ortega doesn't care who he hurts."

Bruce probably sensed the tension in my voice. "You got it, Clint. Don't worry none 'bout Mary Alice. Me and the fellas will take good care of her."

We disconnected and I allowed myself to feel a bit relieved at Bruce's reassuring words. He was a good man and I knew he'd do whatever it took to make sure that Mary Alice was given as much protection as possible. As I sped down the highway, I tried to put the news about Ortega out of my mind, but I couldn't shake the feeling that his escape was going to affect me personally in a very big way.

CHAPTER 9

It was nearly 7:00 PM when I arrived at the Majestic Motor Lodge, situated on the outskirts of Capitol City. I'd chosen it partly because of its out of the way location – I didn't want our work to attract attention. The place was modern and attractive, the rooms were clean and airy, and there was the added attraction of a small lounge and restaurant combination adjacent. *All the comforts of home*, I thought. Well, not really.

The attractive young lady at the front desk, whose name tag identified her as Melissa, informed me that my room was ready and assured me that the charges had been paid in advance, courtesy of the governor's office. She handed me a small packet with the plastic room key and gave me directions to a room on the second floor.

It was actually a small suite with a balcony overlooking the outdoor pool, which offered added benefits on a hot summer day. The room was equipped with a flat screen television, wi-fi, a comfortable sofa, a small bar with refrigerator and microwave oven, and a small one-cup coffee maker with a full supply of coffee packets. The place also had a large bedroom with a second flat screen television, and a spacious bath and shower. I decided that it would do nicely for the next 30 days – hopefully less than that.

I unpacked, put away my things, then called Mary Alice, as promised. She seemed to sense the uneasiness I was feeling and asked me if something was wrong.

"It's been a long drive, and I'm a bit anxious about getting started tomorrow."

"Are you sure that's all?"

Mary Alice would have made a good detective. She could spot a lie a mile away, so I knew here was no use in keeping the truth from her. I had told her when we were first dating about what Ortega had done to my family, and we both slept better knowing that he was in federal custody and would hopefully spend the rest of his rotten life behind bars. Now that he was in the wind, she needed to know that she could be in danger.

I told her what I knew about the situation and asked her to be on the alert for any sign of trouble. "Bruce Johnson will do whatever is needed to see that you are protected. But all the same, please don't take any unnecessary chances."

"You think this Ortega might be headed to Climax?"

"Probably not Ortega himself," I replied, "but maybe one or more of his people. I've asked Bruce to be on alert for any strangers in town. I hope that will be enough, but promise me you'll be extra careful while I'm gone."

"I will, darling," she replied earnestly. "I'm sure I'll be fine. I trust Bruce to keep us all safe here. You just get that job done there and hurry back home."

After a bit of small talk and the exchange of a few words of endearment, I promised to check back with her daily and we disconnected. I felt better after speaking with her and focused on the task at hand. I ran through my mental checklist of things to discuss when my new associates arrived.

As if on cue, my cell phone rang. I didn't recognize the number on the screen, and answered it warily. A man's voice with a pronounced Hispanic accent said, "You Clint?"

I replied that I was, and the caller said, "It's Montijo. Where are you?"

I was caught off guard, but then recalled that Ray Montijo was the name of one of the undercover operatives Nelson Bradford had said would be assigned to work with me. The other one was Alex Arrowsmith. Bradford assured me they were two of the best operatives the state had to offer. Both were absolutely trustworthy, dedicated, and tireless workers. I had to take his word for it; I mentally crossed my fingers and hoped I could count on his judgment.

I recovered quickly and said, "I've just checked into my motel. Where can we meet – and when?"

"We'll come to you," Montijo replied.

I gave him the name and address of the motel and he said, "We'll be there in fifteen minutes."

I finished unpacking and continued thinking about how I could best use Montijo and Arrowsmith in the investigation, but decided that I'd needed to know more about them before I could determine what contribution they could make. While I waited, I brewed myself a cup of coffee – just what I needed after the long, tiring drive.

In less than fifteen minutes, there was a knock on my door. I opened it to find a dark-skinned man, roughly five-feet-five, but powerfully built. I guessed him to be in his mid-30's, but his dark eyes were those of a trained investigator. He wore his hair long and tied in a ponytail and had a thin, dark moustache. He had on reflectorized sunglasses and denim pants, a faded red T-shirt, and a leather vest with tassels hanging down the sides, plus a set of well-worn cowboy boots that had seen better days.

I was surprised to see that his partner was a woman. I'd expected Alex

Arrowsmith to be a man, and this attractive person was most definitely of the female gender. She was utterly striking in appearance, standing an inch or two taller than her companion. Her body was shapely and well-proportioned, with breasts that pushed against a white peasant blouse that clung precariously to her shoulders. Her long raven hair hung down nearly to her waist, and she wore a scarlet ribbon atop her head that complimented her copper-colored skin. She had high cheek bones, piercing dark brown eyes, and the nose of a Roman god. Her mouth was wide and showed perfect teeth when she smiled, as she did when she thrust out her hand to me. Manicured, red-painted toenails could be seen from inside her open-toed sandals. I guessed her to be in her early thirties.

The young woman was the first to speak. "Hi. I'm Alex Arrowsmith, Mr. Harrison. This is my partner, Ray Montijo."

She must have recognized my bewilderment, and quickly explained. "Alex is short for Alexandra, Mr. Harrison. You were probably expecting me to be a man. I hope you're not disappointed."

Surprised, to be sure, but definitely not disappointed, and just a bit embarrassed, to be sure.

"I must admit, you're not what I expected, but –"

She cut in with a cheery laugh. "Yeah, I get that a lot."

I was relieved that she had sense of humor. Montijo's face, on the other hand, remained expressionless.

I ushered them in and invited them to have a seat on the couch, while I took the stuffed chair opposite them.

"Can I offer you coffee or water?"

“No, nothing,” Alex said, apparently the designated spokesperson. “We just wanted to introduce ourselves and discuss a plan of action.”

She was all business, and I liked that. But I wasn’t so sure of Montijo, who seemed to be an observer more than a participant.

“I’m not sure how much the two of you know about why you’re here, or our mission, so let me fill you in on what I know, so we’ll all be on the same page.”

They both nodded. I opened up my laptop, booted it up, and sat it on the coffee table in front of them. “Let me show you what prompted the investigation.”

They sat in silence and watched the video, but the looks on their faces told me they understood the gravity of the situation. When the video flickered off, I said, “The tall man you just saw accepting a packet of money from the other fellow is none other than Captain Lawrence Wilkins, the number two man in the Capitol City Police Department.”

“Geez,” Montijo offered, “I thought I recognized that dude.”

I said, “If this tape is legitimate – and we’ll know that in a day or two – there are serious problems of corruption in the police department.”

Montijo took this in silently.

I went on to point out the political sensitivity of what we’d been asked to do and why the governor had chosen me to take on the assignment.

Alex said, “We know a bit about your background, Sheriff Harrison, and I’d say the governor made a wise decision in bringing you in on this.”

“Well,” I replied, “since you seem to know about me, why don’t you both tell me a little about yourselves.”

I was not surprised when Alex elected to go first. She explained that she was three-fourths Navajo Indian and was born on a reservation in New Mexico. She had worked her way through a small two-year college in Santa Fe, then transferred to New Mexico State College where she had received a degree in computer sciences. She managed to land a job with the New Mexico Department of Revenue as an administrative assistant, and later transferred to their investigative services division where she discovered that she had a talent for computer investigative work. She soon became bored with the investigation of financial crimes and, when she learned about an opening with the Colorado Criminal Investigation Division, Office of Special Operations, she applied, passed the written and oral examinations, and was hired. At that time they desperately needed women investigators, and the fact that she was of native American descent was another factor in her favor.

"I've been with the division for seven years and have worked on a variety of undercover assignments, including one involving a gang of outlaw motorcycle riders who were involved in a series of gas station heists. A major organized crime ring involved in the importation and distribution of crack cocaine. And an illegal sports betting operation that netted more than ten million dollars a month on college and professional sports."

She rattled off these accomplishments matter-of-factly, and I was impressed with her poise and professional experience.

She went on to explain, "Our division is unique in that we have exclusive jurisdiction over any criminal offense we choose anywhere in the state, as long as it falls under certain guidelines. The single exception is any crime that may also be considered a federal offense, such as bank robbery or kidnapping, in which case the FBI has exclusive jurisdiction if they choose to exercise it."

I didn't know much about her agency, and I'd had no direct contact with any of its personnel until now, but I could see that her experience and expertise could be very useful in the investigation we were about to launch.

Alex turned expectantly to Montijo, who stretched out his legs and sprawled comfortably on the couch. In a low, well-modulated voice, Ray said that he'd been with the CID for more than twelve years, and that he'd come directly into the job after serving eight years with the U. S. Marines, where he'd had tours in both Iraq and Afghanistan. He didn't elaborate on his time in the Marines, but something in his eyes told me he'd seen his share of combat on hostile soil. As a former Marine myself, I could relate to what he'd experienced.

Montijo went on to say that he'd worked on some of the same investigations as Alex, but he had also spent three years undercover infiltrating a Mexican gang that was engaged in prostitution, drugs, gambling and several other street crimes in Capitol City. As a result, he had extensive knowledge of the criminal subculture in Capitol City, especially those with roots in the Hispanic community. It was obvious that his experience would be extremely useful in the task at hand.

I had to admit that I was impressed with both of these individuals. They were seasoned investigators and had worked on some top-level cases. The fact that Nelson Bradford was able to come up with two investigators of this caliber underscored how seriously he saw this assignment.

I looked at Alex and said, "I can probably use your help sorting through the maze of information systems, computer files, data bases and spreadsheet programs that I'll be dealing with."

She smiled broadly. "That all depends on what you need – but sure, I'll do what I can."

"At this point, I'm not sure what we'll be dealing with," I replied candidly, "but before we are through with this case, I suspect we'll need someone with a lot more knowledge about computers than I possess. To be honest, I don't know the difference between a megabyte and a Double Whopper, except that I'm pretty sure one is something to eat."

Alex said confidently, "I can help you get inside the department's computer files. I'm familiar with their operating system and I do a little hacking of my own from time to time."

I turned to Ray. "You've done a lot of work here in Capitol City, Ray, and seem to know your way around pretty well."

He gave me a knowing look, but said nothing, so I continued.

"Ray, I'll need you to put feelers out into the community. If there's anything like corruption going on in the CCPD, someone out there is bound to know something about it. I'm sure you have some very good sources of information that may prove useful."

Montijo, the man of few words, said, "Roger that."

"From what we saw on the video," Alex offered, "it sure looks like this Captain Wilkins is the top man in the action. I wonder who else may be involved?"

"It's hard to say," I replied. "The video's very incriminating, that's for sure, but we all know that the truth is sometimes not as obvious as we're led to believe. Especially based on how it came into the governor's possession anonymously. We need to proceed very cautiously and not rush to judgment."

Montijo asked, "So, how do we know if that video is legit – not doctored up? Wouldn't be the first time."

"You're absolutely right, Ray. That's why I've arranged for one of the top men at the FBI lab in Quantico to take a close look at it. I expect to hear something from him in a few days."

Ray and Alex looked at each other then smiled at me.

I explained, "It's my understanding that Chief Ryan and Wilkins are very close, and that it's highly unlikely that Wilkins would be acting on his own in something like this, which could mean that Ryan is involved on some level."

Montijo snorted contemptuously. "Is that something like being sort of pregnant? Seems to me there's no halfway in something like this. Either you're dirty or you're clean."

His point was well taken. We had to be prepared for the worst-case scenario and we all knew it.

"We'll just have to let the investigation take us to whenever it leads us," I said. "We can't start off by making assumptions."

Ray and Alex nodded their agreement.

I went over my "audit" cover story with them, then said, "I'm scheduled to meet with Chief Ryan and one or more of his staff first thing tomorrow morning. The alleged purpose of this meeting is to introduce myself, explain the nature and scope of the 'audit', and what records and personnel I'll need to get started. I'll have a better idea on how to proceed after I've had a day to look things over."

"What do you want us to do while you're poking around inside the police department?" Alex asked. "And how are we going to stay in touch?"

I'd already given this some thought. "Ray, I'd like you to hit the streets and see what information you can pick up from your usual sources. See what you can learn that might suggest protection or anything out of the ordinary. Concentrate on illegal street-level activity that would be most susceptible to protection by corrupt police officers, such as prostitution, drug sales or illegal gambling."

"Will do, boss," he replied.

"Alex, see how much you can find about the records system. I'm sure it's got a lot of security built into it. We may need to crack the system to get what we need."

"That shouldn't be a problem," she said, "I have a friend who has a friend who ... you know."

I didn't really, but I was confident she knew enough to get started. "As for communicating," I said, turning to retrieve a black zippered bag at my feet, "these should work very nicely." I reached in and took out the cell phones Bradford had given me, handed them to Ray and Alex, then explained their functions. "These units are pre-programmed with an automatic speed dial for quicker communication between us," I said. "Speed Dial One rings to all three devices. We use that if we need to talk to each other at the same time. Speed Dial Two goes just to me, Three to Ray and Four to Alex. They also have GPS tracking capability so that we will always know where each of us is, even if we're unable to communicate, and even if the unit is turned off."

I pointed to a small red button on the lower right corner of the unit. "Pay particular attention to this feature. This is your emergency signal. By sliding this small panel to the right and pressing the red button, you automatically activate the emergency notification signal which will be received by the other two units. This tells the others instantly that one of us is in trouble, and this ..." I said as I pointed to a small flashing box on the face of the readout, "gives your exact location. By pressing this same button twice, we will receive a text message directing us to your location."

I looked at my watch and realized that we had been at it for nearly an hour. "I won't keep you any longer," I said. "Let's plan on meeting here again tomorrow evening at six to see what we've got."

"I'll bring the pizza," Ray said as he rose to leave.

"And I'll bring a six-pack," said Alex, following Ray to the door.

As they were leaving, I thought of one more thing. "Remember to keep a low profile. The fewer people who know what we're doing here, the better off we'll all be."

"That's for sure," Alex said and Ray grunted in agreement.

After they left, I thought about the two operators who'd been assigned to me. They definitely fit the image of the "odd couple," but I nevertheless felt very comfortable with them. I really liked their professionalism and can-do attitude. Our meeting left me more confident about our ability to successfully complete the mission.

Before turning in, I called Sam Warden to see if there was any news on Ortega. He had nothing new to report, but assured me that the investigation was their top priority.

Then I called Mary Alice to say goodnight. She promised that she'd be extra careful and on the alert for anything that might suggest Ortega or one of this crew was in the area. I worried about her safety, but I knew she was a smart woman and would be on guard and alert for any sign of danger. It was good to hear her voice and I once again promised her that I'd call her every night. I missed her already, but I had a job to do and was determined to see it through.

CHAPTER 10

I rose early, as I usually do, and drove to police headquarters. On the way, I found an inviting diner and had a very filling pancake breakfast, complete with coffee and a large glass of orange juice. I'd decided to dress in civilian clothes, since I was not there in any official capacity that my uniform might suggest.

I arrived at police headquarters shortly before 8:00 AM, wondering how I would be received by Chief Ryan and his staff. I'd been in law enforcement long enough to know that cops are, by their very nature, cynical and suspicious of "outsiders". This characteristic is reinforced by their training and the culture in which they operate. I learned early in my career that outsiders were not to be trusted, but I hoped that attitude would not impair my meeting with Chief Ryan.

Police stations can be intimidating to the average citizen. Grim-faced men and women, many of them in uniform; some wearing heavy body armor and menacing sidearms, separated from their "clientele" by thick bulletproof glass barriers. This did not convey a sense of welcome or public service. The CCPD headquarters was no exception.

The lobby was alive with humanity when I arrived. A black woman clutching a crying infant was arguing with a uniformed police officer about a parking ticket she'd received "for no damn reason at all," while a toddler in short pants, a dirty T-shirt and a runny nose tugged at her dress and sucked on his thumb. A heavily-tattooed young man with shoulder-length hair and tattered jeans growled loudly at a bored-looking women behind the counter about the cost of getting his car out of the police impound yard. A dark-complected woman was seated at a table poring over a traffic accident form, and talking to herself in Spanish, apparently trying to decipher the instructions for completing the report.

I made my way to the counter and waited for an aging sergeant to glance up from his paperwork. He was in no particular hurry, and when he finally noticed me, he eyed me warily, as if I was about to disturb his routine. He acted like someone who believed that everyone who approached his counter was either ignorant, or a born trouble-maker. His greeting – "Yeah?" – was anything but friendly.

So much for customer relations, I thought.

I produced a smile and asked to be directed to the office of the chief of police. I thought my request might command a little respect, but I was wrong.

"For what?" Despite his rudeness, I did my best to remain tactful. It would do no good to get the locals mad at me my first day on the job.

"I'm Clint Harrison," I said, intentionally omitting my official position. "I have an appointment with Chief Ryan."

The grizzled sergeant scowled, then picked up a telephone, punched in two numbers, mumbled something to himself, then said, "Got a guy here name of Harrison. Says he has an appointment with the boss."

He listened, nodded silently, then hung up and turned back to me. Verification of my appointment with the chief of police didn't seem to impress him. He pointed to an elevator and said, "Fifth floor." Without another word, he returned to his paperwork, his duty done.

I entered the elevator and punched the #5 button, but before the doors closed, two odd-looking characters got on and punched the #4 button. They said nothing, but eyed me warily. I made them for undercover cops, probably working drugs or vice. One was tall and slender and wore faded jeans and a leather vest over a western shirt. A rust-colored beard covered most of his face, and he had cold, grey eyes that seemed to stare at nothing in particular. His companion was short and solid, and looked like a college linebacker. He wore faded jeans and a T-shirt that had a picture of Mighty Mouse on the chest. This one had a shaved head and wore an earring in his right ear. A nasty red scar crawled across his left cheek. A vivid image flashed through my mind as I wondered how he'd gotten it.

Neither of them spoke; instead, both gave me a nasty scowl. The tension in the car was thick enough to cut with a knife as I felt them sizing me up. When we got to the fourth floor, they shot me a hard look before exiting, leaving me wondering if they were members of the police department's welcoming committee.

I exited on the fifth floor and was greeted by a pleasant-looking middle-aged woman. She was a very trim, five-foot three in low heels and wore a navy-blue suit that was molded to the natural curves of her body. Her blonde hair was turning to ashen gray. She made no attempt to conceal its natural color, which only enhanced her beauty. She wore light makeup and her nails were well-manicured and painted a translucent gloss.

"Good morning, Sheriff Harrison," she said warmly. "I'm Valerie Bradley, Chief Ryan's secretary. Please come with me."

We walked down a long hallway and entered a large corner office.

Valerie invited me to be seated in a small waiting room and offered me coffee which I accepted. She left and soon returned with a steaming mug of coffee.

"Cream or sugar?" she asked.

"No thanks." I replied, "I've worked my share of midnights and prefer to take it straight."

She laughed politely, then said, "Chief Ryan is on the phone and will be with you shortly."

With that, she turned and left me alone with my thoughts. I'd never met Chief Ryan, but he had a good reputation around the state. He was known as a progressive, and a staunch advocate of community-oriented policing – a program designed to encourage greater cooperation between the police and various community elements. Something more police departments should take seriously, I thought.

While some police administrators pay lip service to such efforts, Chief Ryan placed his full support behind the program and expected his command staff and the rank and file to fully embrace the concept.

I knew that the CCPD had been awarded several state and national awards for its forward-leaning community policing efforts. More importantly, the department had received relatively little unfavorable publicity in the media on events portraying its officers as brutal, biased, or ruthless. Unfortunately, not all police departments in the state had followed their example.

In less than five minutes, the inner office door opened and Jack Ryan strode in to greet me. I noted that he was relatively short, probably not much more than five-eight, but with the broad shoulders of a weight lifter. His dark hair was cut in a flat top that was a throwback to the sixties. He had a square, determined jaw and a pronounced dimple in the center of his chin. His eyes were dark and piercing and set widely apart under heavy black eyebrows that could stand to be trimmed. He was well-tanned, suggesting that he spent a fair amount of time on the golf course or engaged in other outdoor activity.

Ryan wore a wide smile as he extended his hand in greeting. "Sheriff Harrison, I'm Jack Ryan. It's good to meet you. I've heard a lot about you since that business last year at Heaven's Gate. Welcome to our fair city."

His handshake was warm, firm, and friendly. "Please call me Clint," I offered.

He ushered me into his office and invited me to sit in a comfortable arm chair next to a small coffee table in front of his desk. He came around to sit opposite me, making me feel quite welcome.

As if on cue, Valerie entered and handed him a fresh cup of coffee and offered me a refill.

"I'm good," I replied, and waved her off.

"I'm pleased to have you here, Clint," he said, peering at me from beneath those bushy eyebrows that seemed to dance on his forehead as he spoke.

"Thank you, Chief Ryan," I replied. "I'm looking forward to learning more about how you do business in Capitol City."

I wondered for a moment if he suspected the real purpose of my visit. If so, it would make my job much more difficult.

Ryan looked directly into my eyes and said earnestly, "Clint, this audit is very important to us. We have received more state and federal grant money than any other community in the state, and we're not ashamed of it. We think what we've accomplished with that money is nothing less than spectacular, and I fully expect your audit to reflect that."

I was impressed with the pride in his voice. Chief Ryan was clearly a true believer in the community piloting concept. The feeling was contagious, and I couldn't help wanting to learn more, regardless of my real purpose for being there.

"Well, Chief Ryan," I replied, trying to match his enthusiasm with my own, "I've heard some very exciting things about the programs you've initiated here and I've no reason to doubt the audit will support your claims."

He smiled broadly. "When you review the progress we've made with our advanced technology, you'll see that the money we've received has been well spent. Many of the programs we've developed have served as models for other police agencies."

That was news to me, but I had no doubt that he knew what he was talking about. I admired his enthusiasm for the community policing concept, but I couldn't help wonder if Chief Ryan's enthusiasm was merely a facade intended to mask something much more sinister. Or, was it possible that he didn't know something was going on behind his back?

"My staff has been informed of your visit here and has been instructed to cooperate fully with you. I want you to have the run of the place and to have access to whatever documents or records you might need to fulfill your obligations. I want to be informed if you encounter any difficulty at all in obtaining what you need while you are here."

I was starting to feel a bit uncertain about the scheme in which I was involved. If Chief Ryan was engaged in any illegal activity, or even knew of any, it would be foolish to offer me carte blanche access to all files and records, but that was exactly what he had just promised.

Without warning, a side door opened and a tall, angular man walked in. He wore a well-tailored blue suit, a starched white shirt and a red and blue necktie. His black wing-tip shoes had been polished to a high gloss. The only jewelry visible was an expensive-looking gold wristwatch that must have set him back a week's salary. I struggled to maintain my composure when I realized I was looking at the man I had seen a few days before on a poor-quality, black and white videotape.

I rose to greet the man as Chief Ryan said, also rising, "Clint, I've asked Captain Wilkins to join us."

Captain Wilkins extended his hand and I accepted it, but there was no warmth in the gesture. His dark eyes stared directly into mine as if he was trying to read my inner thoughts.

Chief Ryan went on to say, "Captain Wilkins is one of my most trusted commanders. I've asked him to be your liaison while you're here. He'll be available to assist you with anything you need."

Wilkins produced a thin smile, but I felt an undercurrent of tension between us. I had to accept Chief Ryan at his word. If he had instructed Wilkins to cooperate with me, I figured he'd do just that, Still, after what I'd seen on the video, I didn't feel comfortable with Wilkins, and I decided to be on my guard around him. He was clearly wary of me, and I would probably feel the same way if I was in his place.

"I'm grateful for the assistance," I said, doing my best to appear sincere. Turning to Wilkins, I said, "I'm sure I'll be calling on you from time to time."

He nodded, but said nothing, and continued to stare reservedly at me.

Nelson Bradford had briefed me on Wilkins, who had an impressive resume. At the age of 45, he'd attained one of the most prestigious positions in the CCPD. As the head of the Criminal Investigation Division, he was in charge of one of the most elite and respected units in the entire police department, and he was said to run his division with a firm hand.

Wilkins was seen by many to be the hands-on favorite to step into Chief

Ryan's post when the chief retired in two years. He was totally loyal to his boss, and was known to put the chief's interests above his own. If this was true, it was hard to believe that Wilkins would be involved in any wrongdoing that could eventually injure Chief Ryan as well as seal his own fate. But sometimes truth is stranger than fiction, and I knew by now that almost anything was possible in this business.

Despite his impeccable record, every instinct in my body was telling me that Wilkins was a man to be watched. As I looked into those cold, dark eyes, I realized that working with him over the next few weeks would prove to be a challenge.

Wilkins gestured for me to follow him and said, "If you'll come with me, Sheriff Harrison, I'll show you the office we've set up for you, and I'll go over some of the records we have already pulled for you. I think you'll find that we've anticipated just about everything you'll need while you're here."

Chief Ryan reached out and shook my hand. "Great to have you here, Clint."

I thanked him, then followed Wilkins, who strode quickly down the hallway.

We walked down a long corridor and into a comfortable-looking office equipped with a large oak desk, leather desk chair, two occasional chairs, a file cabinet and a desk console containing a laptop computer, and a printer. A six-button telephone sat on the desk.

"I hope you'll find this acceptable, Sheriff Harrison," Wilkins said, turning to face me.

Wilkins gestured toward the file cabinet, which looked brand new. "You'll find a copy of all of our grant applications for the last five years here, as well as our monthly reports for that period. Our monthly and annual crime and activity reports, and our monthly financial reports, which include an accounting of all grant funds."

He pointed to a large three-ring binder on the desk. "This is a User's Guide for the Management Information System which contains basic instructions for gaining access to the main components of the system, as well as a list of all data files maintained in the system and the codes necessary to access them."

He gave me a quick overview of the system. It seemed simple enough, but I would know more once I attempted to navigate through it.

I couldn't help being impressed. If nothing else, Captain Wilkins was a model of efficiency. He seemed to have anticipated everything that I'd need. I appreciated his thoroughness and told him so. His attitude was brusque and businesslike, and I debated on whether to invite him to call me by my first name, but decided against it. Our relationship, at least for the time being, would continue on a professional basis.

He pointed to a small alcove at the rear of the office that contained a sink, coffee maker and small refrigerator. "You drink your coffee black, I believe, Sheriff Harrison, but there's cream in the cooler and sweetener in the cabinet above if you need it." The man had obviously done his homework, and I found myself wondering how much more he knew about me.

It's furnished better than my own office in Climax, I thought. Chief Ryan is certainly rolling out the red carpet.

"My office is right next door, Sheriff, so please feel free to stop in if you have any questions."

I wondered if placing my office next to his was intended to allow him to keep an eye on me, but, if nothing else, it would certainly help me gain access to him if I needed it.

On his way out the door he turned back to me. "I've instructed my administrative assistant, Donna Sanders, to provide any assistance you may need. Her office is just outside mine. Feel free to ask her if you need anything at all."

I nodded my thanks, thinking that Ms. Sanders might prove useful, but I wondered, Has she been instructed to keep an eye on me and report my every move to Wilkins? For the time being, I'd tread very carefully around Ms. Sanders until I had a better read on her.

After Wilkins left, I sat down at the desk and spent several minutes collecting my thoughts and appraising what I'd experienced since arriving at the police station. Both Chief Ryan and Captain Wilkins had been accommodating, but I needed to feel out Wilkins some more. His apparent cooperation could be a false front to mask a sinister motive. I wouldn't know for sure until I started digging into the organization. If he was merely trying to throw me off the trail, I'd find out soon enough. Meanwhile, I needed to get a better handle on the inner workings of the police department, and that would take some time. I was glad to have Ray and Alex working with me, and was confident that their assistance would be essential as our investigation progressed.

CHAPTER 11

I made myself a pot of coffee and got to work. I began by sorting through and familiarizing myself with the volumes of reports in the file cabinet. I figured it would take me at least an entire day to get through it all. I first needed to make a preliminary assessment of what information I had, then decide what more I might need.

I logged into the computer by using the password I'd been given and entered the department's central records system. I was confronted by a series of classification codes that appeared to cover a wide range of activities, including arrests, offenses, calls for service, and virtually every activity in which members of the police department were engaged. I was confronted with an abundance of statistical data, including crime analysis information, intelligence reports, activity summaries, overtime figures, and so forth.

Most of what was there would probably be of little value to me, but I continued to scan through computer files of every sort imaginable. It was amazing the amount of data that could be stored, analyzed and accessed at the touch of a few keystrokes. I soon became engrossed in learning more than I needed to know about the operations and strategies of the CCPD.

I was lost in thought when I heard a woman's voice. "The coffee smells delicious. May I have some?"

I looked up to see an attractive young woman standing in the doorway holding an empty coffee cup. She was, I guessed, in her mid-thirties. Ginger-colored hair worn in tight curls gave her a funny-girl look. Her horn-rimmed glasses perched on a delicate nose and accentuated her hazel-green eyes. She had on a tight-fitting white blouse and a dark blue skirt that ended just above the knees and revealed shapely legs and trim ankles. She emanated a tantalizing fragrance I couldn't identify.

She flashed a shy smile. "I'm Donna Sanders, Sheriff Harrison.

Captain Wilkins suggested I stop by and introduce myself."

"That was good of him," I said, rising from my seat. "Please help yourself, but fair warning. I tend to make mine rather strong."

She laughed easily and poured herself a cup. "I haven't been working here that long, but I know enough to not be particular about the coffee."

I returned her laugh and extended my hand. "I'm Clint Harrison, here on special assignment. Please have a seat."

She accepted my hand and gave it a warm and firm squeeze, then sat in one of the chairs before my desk. "Yes, Sheriff Harrison, I know who you are and why you're here. I've been instructed to give you any assistance you may need."

I returned to my seat. "That'll be great. I'll need some help finding my way through some of these records," pointing to the files on my desk.

"And please call me Clint."

"All right, Clint, and make it Donna," she returned the offer in kind. "It's not as complicated as you might think, but I'll be happy to help you get started."

Donna put down her cup and proceeded to give me a quick course on the automated records system. After 15 minutes or so I was beginning to understand how the system worked, and it didn't seem nearly as formidable as it had before.

"How do you keep all of this in your head?" I asked. "It seems terribly complicated."

She withdrew a small notebook from her pocket, and chuckled. "Oh, it's not all that hard when you have one of these. I keep everything I need to know written down right here."

"That must come in handy."

"It saves me a lot of time," she nodded. "I'd be lost without my notes."

"Well, I think I have a basic understanding of the system now, but if I run into trouble, I know who to call for help."

She gave me a thumbs-up and rose to go. "I'll be right across the hallway if you need anything, and thanks for the coffee."

"My pleasure," I replied. "I have a feeling I may be calling on you again as I get deeper into the records."

She hesitated, turned back to me and said softly, "Just remember – things are not always what they seem, Clint."

I was about to ask her what she meant by that when the door opened and Captain Wilkins entered. He stared intently at me, then at Donna's retreating form and said, "Well, Sheriff Harrison, has Donna been helping you get the information you need?"

The question was innocent enough, but I couldn't shake the feeling that he was checking up on me. "Yes, she's been very helpful, Captain. I'm doing my best to familiarize myself with your system."

He nodded and said, "It's first rate. I had a hand in designing it." "It's impressive, Captain." I said with all sincerity. "Our record-keeping procedure in Climax is a bit antiquated and I've been trying to get the County Commissioners to give me the money to have it upgraded, but no luck so far."

The hint of a smile played on his lips. "I believe you'll find the User's Guide to be quite helpful, Sheriff. It will tell you just about anything you need to know about the type of data contained in each of the security classifications. I wrote it myself."

"It does seem very user-friendly," I replied, "I've been able to navigate through the system without too much difficulty."

Apparently satisfied that I needed no further assistance, Wilkins turned to leave and reminded me to check with Donna if I needed anything further.

I thanked him and he left without another word. I sat and thought for a while, wondering, Is he monitoring my actions? If so, I'd need to be very discreet about what I said and what I did while under his watchful eyes. He certainly had the capability of planting electronic monitoring devices in my office and could probably track my keystrokes as I maneuvered through the computer files. This would make my job all that more difficult, and I hoped that Alex might have a solution.

I thought about what Donna had said about things sometimes not being what they seem. I wondered how much credibility I could place on the words of a woman I'd just met and about whom I knew next to nothing. If she had useful information, I needed to find a way to get it from her. Perhaps I could meet her somewhere she'd feel more comfortable. I decided to give to give this possibility more thought.

I spent several more hours poring through a variety of electronic files and finding nothing even remotely suspicious. The deeper I dug into the department's offense and arrest records, the more immersed I became. One of the things I noted with interest was the unusually high clearance rates for some of the major offenses, such as homicide, rape and robbery. The department's clearance rate, which meant the percentage of cases "cleared" by arrest or other investigative means was between 70 and 80 percent for these major offenses. Even the clearance rate for so-called "vice crimes," such as drugs and prostitution, was quite high. I knew that such statistics do not come about easily, and usually resulted from good, old-fashioned police work and tireless effort by detectives and undercover operators. Another indication that the CCPD's reputation as one of the best in the country was well-deserved, I thought.

As I worked, I couldn't shake the feeling that my every move was being monitored. Finally, after skipping lunch, I realized that I'd been at it for nearly eight solid hours. It was after 4 PM and my eyes were blurry from staring at the computer for so long. I'd accomplished very little and decided to call it a day. My next move was to reach out to Ray and Alex, hoping they'd have news that would buoy my spirits and help move our investigation forward. I sent a text message to Alex reminding her that I'd meet her and Montijo at my hotel in an hour. She responded almost immediately and said they'd be there.

I was about to leave when my cell phone rang. I looked at the screen and saw Sam Warden's number. Wanting to take his call in private, I answered and said, "Sam, let me call you back in five minutes," then disconnected.

Once outside, I called Sam back as I reached my car. Hoping for good news, I asked, "Sam, have you got him? Is Ortega back in jail where he belongs?"

"Uh, no, Clint, not exactly."

My heart skipped a beat. "What do you mean, 'not exactly,' Sam? Do you have him or not?"

"What I mean, Clint," he said tentatively, "is that we don't one-hundred percent have Ortega, but we have something – or someone – who we believe is Ortega."

His words made no sense. "Please explain, Sam."

"Just about an hour ago, I got a call from the L. A. County Bomb and Arson Task Force. There was an explosion in a home in East L.A., and they recovered a body. We have reason to believe it is Ortega."

"Ortega? Killed by a bomb?" It was hard to believe, but it would be poetic justice if true, since he was personally responsible for the bomb that killed my family. But it was also very convenient. "Sam, are you absolutely sure it's Ortega?"

"No, Clint, at this point we cannot be sure, but all the signs point to it being him. There wasn't much left to identify, but we did find some evidence at the scene that would tend to confirm his identity – driver's license, credit cards, etcetera."

That wasn't much, and I knew it. Sam probably did too. "What about dental records, fingerprints, DNA?"

"We're still working on all that," he replied hopefully, "but the blast was so great that the recovery team doesn't have much to work with."

I had serious doubts about the situation, but knew it was best to hold out hope until a conclusive ID of the body could be made.

"We spoke with neighbors who confirmed seeing someone who looked like Ortega, and one or two others going into the house shortly before the blast occurred."

"Were they able to make a positive ID?"

"We showed them photos, but they couldn't be sure it was him. We think this was a safe house he was using until he could make his next move."

I tried to keep my disappointment from showing. "Anything else?" "We did find some charred bits of clothing that may be prison fatigues. We're hoping the lab boys may be able to positively determine that they're from the prison. If we're lucky, they may even find some DNA they can match with Ortega."

"What about the bomb?" I asked.

"The bomb and arson guys are pretty sure it was C-4. They found fragments of blasting caps in the rubble. We're sending it all to the lab for analysis. We should know something in a day or so."

"Please keep me posted, Sam," I said.

"You bet, Clint. Just as soon as I know anything, you'll know."

I thanked him for the call and disconnected, unsure what to think. Ortega's death – if that's what it was – solved a very big problem for me. It was a very fitting end for a cold-blooded monster.

I headed to the motel, hoping I'd heard the last of Carlos Ortega. I did my best to clear my mind of thoughts about what I'd just learned and focus on the mission ahead. Hopefully, Ray or Alex would have something useful to tell me.

CHAPTER 12

When I arrived at the hotel, Alex and Montijo were waiting for me and we went inside. When they were both seated, I offered cold beer and they accepted gratefully. I opened one for myself and said, "Tell me something good."

To my surprise, Montijo was the first to speak. "I definitely think we're onto something here, Clint. Normally I can round up a truckload of snitches if I work hard at it, but most of them don't want to be found and the few I did find are not talking."

"Maybe they're just shy," I said, smiling.

"Oh, believe me, they have plenty to say when they want to, especially if the money's right."

Alex offered, "They're not talking either because they are afraid to, or because it's worth a lot more to keep quiet."

"If they're afraid to talk," I said thoughtfully, "there must be some very powerful people who're intimidating them."

Montijo said, "That's what I think too. The real question is, who has that kind of power?"

"That's the sixty-four-dollar question," Alex said, taking a sip of her beer.

"Well," I said, trying to remain optimistic, "it may mean that we're on the right track. We just have to keep digging."

I asked Alex, "What about you? Any luck?"

"Not really, Clint," she replied, "but I did manage to pick up one small bit of information that may prove useful. I ran into a friend of mine who clerks at the Superior Court. Her boss is Judge Hiram Wiley, who gets most of the big drug cases assigned to him. She said that there seems to be an unusually high number of major drug cases getting kicked out, either during the preliminary hearing or on arraignment."

This got my attention. "Is that unusual?"

Alex shrugged. "She says that most of the cases are being kicked for obvious problems with the arrest, or with search and seizure issues. Officers not having sufficient probable cause, failing to advise a defendant of his Miranda rights – that sort of thing."

"Sounds like sloppy police work," Montijo said. "Cops take short cuts, sometimes even fabricate evidence, thinking the ends justify the means, then blame the court when their cases are kicked out. Happens all the time, you know."

"Yeah, Ray, I know," Alex agreed, "but this is different. Most of these cases are being made by a joint city-county task force, and these guys know better. My friends said it's almost like they were making the mistakes on purpose just so the case would never go to trial."

This information didn't agree with what I'd learned earlier about the unusually high clearance rate for drug cases. There was an obvious disconnect between what the police department's records said and what both Ray and Alex were picking up on the street. I shared what I knew with them and asked, "Does that make sense?"

Both shook their heads.

"There must be an error in their records," Alex suggested.

"But it's supposed to be a state-of-the-art system," I said. "I just can't understand how the statistics can be wrong." I addressed Alex, "Is there any chance you can get access to those court records for, say, the last six months? Maybe we'll find a pattern."

She grinned. "Somehow, Clint, I knew you were going to ask me that, and I'm one step ahead of you. My friend owes me a favor and I managed to sneak a peek at the access code for the online database that carries all of the court's transactions."

"Which means that you – "

"Which means that I," she said triumphantly, "and my trusty little laptop, can browse to my heart's content through those court records. Just what did you want to know?"

Before I could reply, the bedside phone chimed, startling me. I didn't expect any calls on this phone.

I picked up the receiver. "Hello?"

A female voice asked, "Sheriff Harrison?" The voice was familiar, but I couldn't readily place it.

"Yes?"

"This is Donna Sanders, Sheriff Harrison. I hope you don't mind me calling you."

"No, of course not," I assured her. "But how did you know how to reach me?"

She hesitated, then said, "Your room key was on your desk. I saw the name of the hotel on it."

I remembered that I'd tossed my room key along with my car keys there.

"You're very observant, Donna," I said. "You'd make a good detective. Now what can I do for you?"

Alex and Ray exchanged curious looks, but said nothing.

"Can we meet somewhere privately?" she asked. "I have something to tell you and I ... well, I don't want to discuss this with you at work."

My curiosity was in overdrive, and I sensed tension in her voice. "Yes, certainly. When and where?"

She paused for a moment, then said, "How about Charley O's? It's quiet and out of the way."

I agreed, and she said she'd meet me there in an hour. The connection was broken and I stared at Alex and Ray.

"Sounds like you've got a date, Clint," Ray said, grinning broadly. "Not really, but maybe a lead," I said. "I'll know more in an hour."

I turned to Alex. "See if you can get those court records, including the names of the officers involved and the names of the suspects."

Then, "Work with Alex to see if you can detect any kind of pattern, particularly involving the same officers. You might find nothing, but it's the best thing we've got going right now."

As they rose to leave, I said, "Let's plan on getting together tomorrow, same time. Call me if you dig up something hot before then."

After they left, I had just enough time to take a quick shower and change into something more casual. I Googled the address of Charley O's, punched it into my car's navigation system, and headed out.

On the way there, I continued to be troubled by the apparent conflict between what I'd learned in my review of the department official records, and what Alex and Ray were learning from their contacts on the street. Could the records somehow be wrong – or even falsified? For what purpose? And by whom?

My thoughts shifted to Donna Sanders, and I felt a surge of excitement, hoping what she had to tell me would get the investigation headed in the right direction.

CHAPTER 13

I made it to Charley O's a few minutes before 8:00 PM, my scheduled meeting time with Donna Sanders. The restaurant was perched on a hilltop with a majestic view of the city. The sun was just slipping behind the mountains to the west and the view of the snow-capped peaks was spectacular. The parking lot was full, attesting to the popularity of the place, and the delicious aroma wafting from inside reminded me that I hadn't eaten in hours.

The bar was crowded, but I managed to find a small table in the far corner and made my way there after informing the woman at the front desk where I'd be, and asking her to direct Donna Sanders there when she arrived. A waitress approached and offered me a menu, and I informed her I was waiting for someone, but ordered a beer. Sinatra was crooning in the background. I sat quietly, soaking up the atmosphere and relaxing. It had been a long day spent accomplishing very little, so I was anxious to learn what Donna had to tell me.

By 8:15, I'd finished my drink and Donna still hadn't shown. I dialed her cell phone, but got only her voicemail. I ordered a second beer, but an uneasy feeling in my stomach kept me from enjoying it. By 8:30, I'd made two more unsuccessful calls to Donna, and I was beginning to think she wasn't going to show. I thought about driving by her place, then realized I had no idea where she lived. One more unanswered call to her cell phone convinced me that the much-anticipated meeting was not going to happen. I paid my tab and made my way to my car as I tried to ward off a feeling of dread that wrapped around me like a cold, heavy blanket.

On the way back to my hotel, I wondered what could have caused Donna to cancel out on our meeting. I couldn't shake the feeling that something bad had happened – or was about to happen. As I approached my room, I noticed one of the cleaning women pushing her cart down the sidewalk. I thought this odd, since I knew that the housekeeping crew rarely worked this late.

Once inside my room, I stripped off my clothes, and turned on the shower, allowing the stinging jets of water to massage my body and refresh my spirit. But the nagging concern about Donna Sanders' failure to show up for our meeting continued to bother me. Perhaps she'd have an explanation when I saw her at the office in the morning.

I stepped from the shower and reached for a towel, only to discover that there were no clean towels to be found. Cursing softly, I grabbed the telephone from the desk, and dialed Operator.

A man answered on the third ring, and I explained my problem to him.

"Can you send someone from housekeeping down with some fresh towels? They seem to have missed my room."

There was a momentary pause, then he said, "Uh, Mr. Harrison, housekeeping left hours ago, but I can have Harry, the maintenance guy, bring you some."

His words jolted me like an electric shock, and I immediately thought about the cleaning lady I'd seen outside my room minutes before.

"What kind of uniforms do your housekeeping crew wear? Is it a black skirt with a white blouse?" I knew the answer, but I wanted to confirm my suspicion.

"Well, no sir, Mr. Harrison. All of our housekeeping girls wear a pink skirt and pink blouse with a white apron. Did you still want me to have –"

I threw the receiver back on the cradle and stared at it, thinking about what to do next. My impulse was to run out in pursuit of the "cleaning lady", but by this time she'd be long gone.

My thoughts were interrupted by a loud knock on the door. I quickly slipped on a pair of pants and opened it to find a large, burly man in coveralls – probably Harry – handing me a stack of towels. I thanked him; he left without a word, and I closed the door behind him.

My cell phone rang and I grabbed it, hoping it was Donna calling with an explanation. Instead, it was Alex.

"Hi Clint," she said. "How did your meeting with Donna Sanders go?"

"It didn't," I said, and filled her in on the details.

"That's strange," she said. "What do you think it means?"

"I have no idea, but I've got a bad feeling about this. She acted like she had something really important to tell me. I tried to call her several times, but she didn't pick up."

Then I told her about the mysterious cleaning woman.

I heard her say something to Montijo; then she said to me, "Just sit tight, Clint. We'll be right there."

Before I could respond, she disconnected. While I waited for them to arrive, I got dressed, then turned on the television to catch the evening news. In less than ten minutes, they were at my door. I muted the television and invited them in.

Montijo carried a small leather satchel under his arm. Without a word, he set it down and withdrew a device that I guessed was some kind of electronic monitoring instrument. He seemed to know exactly what he was doing, and Alex and I watched silently. He motioned for Alex and I to remain quiet while he worked.

Meanwhile, we watched as Montijo removed the mouthpiece from the bedside telephone. He withdrew something that looked like a ceramic button, and held it up triumphantly. Motioning both of us to remain silent, he threw it to the floor and stomped on it with his boot.

Thirty minutes and two electronic monitoring devices later, he declared the room to be clean, so we could talk.

"That's some real fancy stuff," he said, pointing to the pile of smashed bugs on the floor.

"Oh yeah?"

"You bet," he said resolutely. "Probably made in China, but very high-tech. I'd say we're up against some big players, no question 'bout that."

"Well," Alex offered, "whoever's listening in on you will know now that we're onto them."

"That's for sure," I answered, "but it doesn't get us any closer to knowing who it is. I'd hoped Donna might be able to provide this information."

Alex asked, "Clint, did you check to see if anything is missing?"

I admitted that I hadn't, and began to do just that. In a few minutes I was reassured that nothing had been taken.

"What about your cell phone and your laptop?"

"No, I had those with me. There's really nothing else that would interest anyone."

My voice trailed off as I glanced at the television and was shocked to see the image of none other than Donna Sanders on the screen. Beneath the photo, a caption read: "Capitol City police employee fatally injured in crash."

I stared at the screen, struggling to deal with the reality of what I saw.

Alex must have read the stark horror in my eyes. She grabbed the remote and adjusted the sound. We watched in stunned silence as the wreckage of an overturned car was shown lying on its side on a mountain road. The scene was illuminated by the flashing lights of several police cars, a tow truck, as a gurney with a covered body was loaded onto a fire department rescue vehicle.

According to the reporter, Donna Sanders had been killed in a one-car traffic accident just before 8:00 PM that evening. The crash had occurred on a remote highway west of the city as she traversed a grapevine curve. A preliminary investigation suggested that brake failure may have contributed to the accident as there were no skid marks. A highway patrolman, who was first on the scene, theorized that the car was traveling at a high rate of speed. The car broke through a guard rail and smashed into a bridge abutment, causing massive head and internal injuries to the driver, despite the use of body restraints. One look at the wrecked car was enough to convince anyone that it would have taken a miracle to survive such a crash. The highway patrolman investigating the accident was quoted as saying, "This particular stretch of highway can be extremely hazardous due to the number of hairpin curves that must be safely navigated."

Alex muted the television and said, "Now we know why she didn't show up for your meeting."

I wondered, How is this possible? Is Donna's death a mere coincidence? Could there be a more sinister explanation?

As if reading my mind, Alex said, "Do you think it's possible that her death is somehow related to our investigation?"

"Good God, I hope not," I said, "but it certainly makes me suspicious."

"Yeah, no shit," Montijo replied dolefully.

Alex asked, "So where do we go from here, Clint?"

"I'm not sure," I said. "Somehow, we need to find out if this was simply a tragic accident or something else."

Ray chimed in, "I think I may be able to help with that."

Alex and I looked expectantly at Ray. He explained, "My cousin Felipe works for the highway patrol. He's in their accident reconstruction unit. I'll give him a call tomorrow and see what I can find out."

"That'll be a big help," I said.

"Yeah," Alex commented, "but even if we find out that her accident wasn't an accident, it still doesn't tell us if it had anything to do with our investigation."

"One thing for sure," Ray said, "is that we'll never know what Donna thought was so important to tell you."

"Yes," Alex said, "we're right back where we started."

"Not necessarily," I shrugged. Ray and Alex looked at me expectantly.

"Donna showed me a notebook," I explained. "She said she kept everything in that notebook."

Alex asked, "You think what she had to tell you might be in there?"

"It's possible," I said. "And I'll bet she had that notebook with her when her car crashed." I turned to Ray. "What's the chance of retrieving that notebook?"

Ray thought for a moment, then said, "Well, anything like that found at the scene would be tagged and turned into Property Control. I'll check with Felipe. He'll know who to ask about it."

Great," I replied.

"I'll see if I can find a way to backdoor the police department's computer files," Alex offered.

"Let's get together tomorrow to compare notes," I suggested. "Where and when?" Alex asked.

"You know the city better than I do. What do you suggest?"

Alex looked at Ray, who winked at her and asked, "You like Mexican?"

"Traditional?" "You bet," he said.

"Sounds good to me," I replied. "Where?"

Alex gave me the name and address of a place called Casa Cortez, and we agreed to meet there at 6:00 PM the following evening.

When they rose to leave, I said, "Listen. Donna's death may be no accident, and the fact that someone has planted bugs in my room means that we have to be extra careful. Our lives could be in danger."

They both nodded, and the look in their eyes told me they recognized the potential danger we faced.

"Take no chances and stay alert at all times."

"You got it, Clint," Ray said.

They left and I sat down on the sofa and thought about the situation. Although we had nothing to show for our effort, it was very possible that our actions were making someone very nervous. Hopefully, this might lead that same someone to make a serious mistake that would turn the tide of events in our favor.

I was startled by the ringing of my cell phone and realized I hadn't called Mary Alice as I'd promised. She chided me gently for the oversight, and I was careful not to mention Donna's death. She, on the other hand, was in good spirits, and even bragged a bit about the progress being made by Jennifer, the new girl.

"She's actually quite nice," May Alice said. "I think she'll work out just fine."

I was happy that she was in such a good mood, and it helped to bolster my own spirits. A few minutes later we said goodnight. Despite my wariness, I knew that sleep would probably not come easily. I took a cold bottle of beer from the refrigerator and slipped through the TV channels until I settled on a rerun of Gunsmoke. Marshall Dillon had always been one of my heroes.

CHAPTER 14

Due to the events of the previous evening, I'd had a fitful sleep, but was up at the crack of dawn all the same. I arrived early at the CCPD headquarters, hoping to get to my office without running into Captain Wilkins. His very presence made me uneasy, and I knew I'd be able to get more done without having his watchful eyes checking my every move. But he was waiting for me when I arrived, and I wondered if he'd ever left.

I greeted him politely and he returned the favor, but I sensed something different in his demeanor. The cold stare was gone, replaced by something very different.

"I suppose you've heard about Donna," he said solemnly. The cool, business-like tone was now tempered with a touch of sadness. It was an emotion I hadn't thought him capable of. Just 24 hours earlier he'd seemed the epitome of calculating indifference. Now, the empathy in his voice was palpable. If he'd had anything to do with Donna's death, there was certainly no hint of it as he stood before me.

"Yes, I did," I replied sadly. "What a horrible tragedy. Have you learned anything on the investigation?"

He shook his head and waved me into his office, directing me to a chair opposite his desk.

"Coffee?" He offered me a cup from a decanter behind his desk, and I readily accepted, grateful for the friendly overture.

"We don't know much more than they reported last night," he said wearily. "It appears to be a horrible accident, but the state's accident reconstruction team is handling the investigation."

I knew this already, but didn't reply.

"I found her to be a very capable and engaging young woman," I said. "Does she have family here? What about children?"

He shook his head again and sipped his coffee. "No, no family that I know of. She moved here two years ago from Indiana. I believe she'd been married and divorced at a very early age."

There was silence for a moment, then he said, "I've got another woman coming in to take Donna's place temporarily. She's Bob Mortimer's secretary. Bob's on vacation for a month, so Marilyn Means – that's her name – will be helping us out here for a while. I'll send her in to see you when she arrives."

Our conversation seemed to be over, so I excused myself and returned to my office, still wondering about the nature of this man, Wilkins. It was possible that there was more to him than was evident. And I wished I knew how to peel off the veneer and unveil the true man.

I made myself a pot of coffee and settled in to resume my review of the stack of reports. Time passed quickly and it was nearly noon when my cell phone rang. I glanced at the dial and my heart skipped a beat when I saw that it was Mary Alice. She wouldn't be calling me during business hours unless it was something important.

I answered, and the hysteria in her voice put me on instant alert. "Oh, God.

Oh my God! It's terrible! I can't believe it. That poor girl. Oh my God, I..."

"What is it?" I asked, fighting to keep myself under control. My hands were shaking and I spilled coffee on myself, indifferent to the pain it inflicted.

Finally, she managed to say, "It's Jennifer, Clint. The new girl. She's ... dead. It's horrible." Then she broke into sobs again. The image of the young waitress flashed into my mind.

The sobbing continued and I waited, feeling her pain. Finally, I said, "Please, sweetheart, calm down. Tell me what happened."

Her crying subsided and she took a deep breath. "It's all my fault, Clint. If I hadn't..."

I struggled to keep my own emotions under control. "What do you mean, it's your fault, Mary Alice? I don't understand."

Before she could answer, my cell phone beeped and I looked at the screen. It was Bruce Johnson calling, and I guessed he had more bad news for me, but that would have to wait. Right now, Mary Alice needed me and she was my top priority.

I still didn't understand what she was trying to tell me. "What do you mean, it's all your fault?"

Finally, she managed to say, her voice trembling, "Jennifer's car is in the shop and I loaned her my car to run a quick errand while she was on her break. That's when it happened. Oh my God, Clint ..." She broke into sobs again.

"That's when what happened?"

"The explosion," she managed to say. "Oh Clint, I feel so terrible." The realization of what she'd said sent a cold chill down my spine.

"What kind of explosion, Mary Alice? I don't understand."

She sniffed, then let it all out. "Seconds after she left, we heard this deafening blast at the rear of the restaurant. Sherman ran out to investigate, then ran back inside and told me to stay put while he called the fire department. By the time they arrived, there was nothing they could do."

She started crying again. "Oh Clint, I feel so horrible. If only I hadn't ..."

I searched for words to console her, but I was having difficulty dealing with the enormity of the situation itself. I offered, "I know you've had a terrible experience, but thank God you're okay. Now, I've got to call Bruce Johnson back. But first I need you to get yourself under control. Just stay there with Sherman and I'll call you right back."

She promised to do as I asked. I disconnected, then called Bruce back. He picked up after the first ring.

I asked, "What do you have, Bruce?"

"It's a real mess, Clint," Bruce said, his voice trembling. "I've never dealt with anything quite like this. There wasn't much left of that poor girl to identify her, but we have an eyewitness who saw her in the car just before the explosion. There's not much doubt it was her. I'm told her name was Jennifer Moore. She worked at the café with ..."

He paused, unable to go on, and a sickening feeling grew in my stomach. I'd only met Jennifer once. She seemed like a real nice girl, and Mary Alice had been warming to her, despite her early misgivings about her work habits.

I already knew the answer, but I asked anyway. "Bruce, was it a car bomb?"

He let out a deep sigh. "Looks like it, Clint. But we won't be sure until the bomb and arson boys get here – maybe later today."

"Who do you have coming?"

"Dave Corrigan from the State Police Bomb and Arson Squad for sure. And ATF says they'll send one of their guys out to lend a hand. In the meantime, our guys will protect the crime scene."

It was about all he could do at that point, and I told him so. But I wanted more than anything to be there myself to make sure that Mary Alice was safe. Bruce was a capable man, but he'd never been up against anything like this, and I felt an urgent need to look after Mary Alice personally. "Bruce," I said, "maybe I should come down there. I'm concerned about Mary Alice. She's pretty shaken up by this."

There was a pause while Bruce thought this over. Then he said, "Well, Clint, that's your call, but I really don't think it's necessary. We can handle things on this end. You don't need to worry none about Mary Alice. Me and Edna will take good care of her."

Edna was Bruce's wife and just as solid and dependable as Bruce. She was a former Army nurse and knew how to deal with tough situations. It was comforting to know that Mary Alice was in capable hands.

I thought about it for a minute and decided he was right. Being with Mary Alice would make me feel better, but wouldn't serve any useful purpose. I'd made a promise to the governor, and I needed to see it through. I took a deep breath and said, "Well, okay, Bruce. I know you're doing all you can. Look after Mary Alice for me and call me the minute you learn anything I should know."

The likelihood that a bomb had been planted in Mary Alice's car left no doubt in my mind that Carlos Ortega was taking out his revenge on me by attacking the most important person in my life. This realization sickened me. I knew Ortega would keep on trying until he accomplished what he set out to do – or until someone stopped him.

But how could Ortega even know about Mary Alice? I asked Bruce this and he thought he might have an answer.

"Well, Clint," he said, "I spoke with Sherman and he told me there was a rough-lookin' fella in the café day before yesterday asking a bunch of questions about you."

This didn't sound good. "What kind of questions?"

"Oh, you know, who you were, were you in town, that kinda stuff." My heart sank and I asked, "And what did Sherman tell him?" Bruce sighed, then said, "Well, Clint, you know Sherman: Telephone, teletype, tell Sherman. Not much better way to get news around town than to tell Sherman."

He was right. Sherman had a reputation for passing along every bit of gossip he heard. He didn't mean anything by it, but everyone in town knew not to trust Sherman with any information they didn't want to get around.

"You get a description of this guy?"

"You bet I did." Bruce said. "I put out the word to the fellas on the street to pick him up if they see him, but my guess is he's long gone by now."

That was probably true. I knew Carlos Ortega wasn't about to leave a trail that would lead back to him.

"Bruce, let's see if Sherman can help our local sketch artist, Jean Dixon, put together a likeness of this guy."

"Will do," Bruce replied, "but what then?"

"Then, let's get the sketch out to the state and federal investigators.

Maybe we'll get lucky."

I shared my suspicions about Ortega with Bruce. "Ortega may have arranged for this hit, but he wouldn't come himself. The chances of tracking the bomber down are slim and none, but it's still worth the effort."

"Meanwhile," I said, "I'll check with Sam Warden in L. A. to see if they've made any progress in the investigation of that home explosion."

When I was satisfied that things were as good as could be expected on that end, we disconnected. Then I placed a call to Sam Warden. "What do you have, Sam?"

"Not much, I'm afraid, Clint, but I can tell you with reasonable certainly that the body we found in the rubble of that explosion in L. A. was not Ortega. We're not sure who it was – probably some homeless derelict – but the county lab boys ran a DNA match and we can rule Ortega out for sure."

My worst fears had just been confirmed. Ortega was very much alive, which meant that my life and the lives of people I cared about – especially Mary Alice – were very much in danger.

I started to fill Sam in on the events in Climax, but he was already on it. "I've got Cynthia Delgado from our Santa Fe office on her way there. She'll be coordinating with the state bomb and arson investigators and your deputy, Bruce Johnson. She'll let me know the minute they have anything useful."

That made me feel a bit better. I thanked him and disconnected. Then I sat for a while, thinking about all that had happened in the last 24 hours and wondered what was yet to come.

I called Mary Alice back and asked, "Are you all right, sweetheart?"

"Yes, my love," she replied, seeming much more composed. "I'm fine. It was just such a shock that I ..."

"I know," I said. "It's awful, but I'm just relieved to know you're okay. I spoke to Bruce and he's got things under control there. He said he'd have Edna look in on you if you need someone."

"Yes, she's here with me now. You don't need to worry about me. I just wish you were here. I feel so ..."

I felt terrible about not being there to protect her, but I knew she was in good hands. As much as I wanted to shield her from the truth, I knew I must level with her and tell her about Ortega. She already knew about the bomb that had killed my wife and young son, so there was no point in not sharing with her my worst fears. If she found out later that I hadn't been honest with her about the danger he posed, she might never forgive me, and I just couldn't let that happen.

So, I filled her in on my suspicions about Ortega, and I was relieved that she took it quite calmly. Finally, she said, "Well, I know you're concerned about my safety, Clint, but I'm in good hands with Bruce and Edna. And now that I know about this man, Ortega, I'll be extra careful. Meanwhile, you finish up the job the governor gave you and get back to me as soon as you can."

Her attitude was reassuring, and I felt better after talking with her. I promised to call her daily to make sure she was all right. We said goodbye and disconnected. In the meantime, Carlos Ortega posed a serious threat, but worrying about him would accomplish nothing. I had more than enough to occupy my thoughts here in Capitol City.

CHAPTER 15

After learning about the events in Climax, it was difficult to think about anything else, but I did my best to concentrate on the files Wilkins had given me.

I turned my attention to the computer files I'd examined the day before. Most of the records were of no interest to me, but I was still puzzled by some of those mysterious classifications codes I'd stumbled onto. I hoped Alex would have an answer for me the next time we talked.

By lunchtime, my stomach was still in knots, worrying about the situation at home. I had no appetite, so instead of eating, I reviewed some of the grants that the CCPD had received over the years. It was an impressive record. In just over ten years, the CCPD had raked in several million dollars in both state and federal grants – perhaps more than any other city of its size in the United States. Many of these grants were for hardware and equipment – bulletproof vests, body-worn cameras, night-vision surveillance gear, and the like, but others were for some more creative and innovative programs dealing with alternative to traditional policy strategics.

One program in particular caught my eye, and I read with fascination the details of the grant. The Community Outreach Program was rather unique in that it embraced a number of social service initiatives dealing with such things as homelessness, unemployment and under-employment, below standard schools, and other issues not normally considered to be within the purview of a law enforcement agency.

Under the Community Outreach Program, the CCPD interfaced with diverse community, criminal justice and social service agencies, hospitals, halfway houses, drug clinics, employment agencies, and mental health institutions to address the underlying issues that contribute to crime and lawlessness in the urban ghetto.

While the program had yet to prove itself – it was still in the first year of a planned three-year effort – it had more than its share of supporters; but many detractors as well. Those who failed to see the value of the program were some of the more hardline members of the community, and the political structure, who groaned about spending too much money on "pie in the sky" social theories. Some critics claimed that the money should go toward proven crime-fighting techniques, such as increased patrol efforts. One of the loudest critics was Tom Bogart, president of the local chapter of the Fraternal Order of Police. Bogart proclaimed that, while the government was willing to spend huge sums of monies in "crackpot theories," the real needs of the police department – more manpower, equipment and financial support – were being ignored. Even State's Attorney David Duncan, who was related to Chief Ryan, had expressed some strong reservations about the program. But not enough to turn off the spigot of federal monies that seemed to flow nonstop into the CCPD.

The program was headed up by Commander Lanson Underwood, who appeared to be a rising star in the CCPD. According to the newspaper article I found in the file, which contained a recent photo of Underwood, he was the perfect choice to head up the program. A former Iraq combat veteran, he was young, black, good-looking, and well-educated. Before joining the CCPD, Underwood had earned both his Bachelors and Masters degrees. He had risen rapidly through the ranks and had an impressive track record of success in the Narcotics Bureau, the Organized Crime Unit, and in the Professional Standards Division. He was also a recent graduate of the prestigious FBI

National Academy, one of the premier executive level training programs in law enforcement.

The more I read about the program, the more interested in it I became; and I made a mental note to see if I could meet with Commander Underwood in person, and get a firsthand account of what his program was doing, along with any early progress reports.

I became so engrossed in learning about the enormous potential of the Community Outreach grant that I lost track of time and was startled when my cell phone rang. I glanced at the screen and saw that it was Herb Jensen from Quantico.

"Working late Herb? Hopefully not on my account." It was nearly seven o'clock in Virginia, and I felt a little bad thinking that he as putting in long hours for me.

"You know me, Clint. I've never been a clock watcher." "That's for sure, Herb. What do you have for me?"

Herb cleared this throat, then said, "Well, I can tell you for certain that the videotape you sent me has been doctored. But they actually did a pretty good job of it."

I perked up. "Meaning what?"

"Well," he replied, "without high-resolution micro-optics, you'd never know the difference. But with the technology we have, the alteration is pretty obvious. They've managed to put this guy Wilkins' voice and image into the picture and make it look like it's really him saying those words. But it's not him at all."

When I realized the impact of what Herb was saying, I asked, "So the obvious question then is, who doctored the video and why?"

"You bet," Herb responded. "But I can't help you on that."

"I know, Herb, but I appreciate what you've done. Now I've got some work to do on my end."

We disconcerted, and I thought about what I'd just learned. Someone was trying to make Captain Wilkins look like he was connected with criminal activity. But who would stand to gain by that? And why? These questions now took central stage in our investigation.

It was time to bring Ray and Alex into the loop on this new turn of events. By five-thirty I'd grown weary of poring over the computer printouts Wilkins had given me and my appetite had returned. I closed up shop and retrieved my car from the parking lot and plugged the address Alex had given me into my GPS. On the way, I used my Bluetooth to call Bruce Johnson. He told me that Jean Dixon had put together a decent sketch of the stranger Sherman had spoken to the day before the explosion.

"I got copies out all over town." Bruce said. "Maybe we'll get lucky and find someone who can put this fella at the scene."

"Keep at it, Bruce," I said. "Anything else?"

"Well, I've got copies out to the state and federal guys too. Maybe that'll help."

"Yeah, maybe," I said without much enthusiasm. I knew Bruce was doing everything he could, but I also knew that Ortega was very cagey and not one to leave loose ends.

"What else?"

"Well, the Bomb and Arson squad did determine that the explosion in Mary Alice's car had been triggered by a detonator activated by the car's ignition switch. But they said that's not very original."

I grew sick to my stomach when I recalled the bomb that had killed my wife and son two years before. That bomb had been activated in the same way.

"No, I suppose it's not," I agreed. "But originality was never Carbos Ortega's strong suit." My heart went out to that innocent young girl who had been killed by the vengeful act of a bloodthirsty killer, and I vowed to exact my own revenge on Ortega for what he'd done.

I asked Bruce once again to keep a close eye on Mary Alice for me, and he assured me he would. We disconnected just as I arrived at the address Alex had given me. It wasn't all that impressive from the outside, but I was hungry and anxious to share what I knew with Ray and Alex, and hoped they'd have something useful as well.

CHAPTER 16

Casa Cortez was located in an older part of the city, populated by small, single-family homes, mom and pop grocery stores, and a scattering of other small businesses. It had definitely seen better days, and I questioned their choice of restaurants as I parked my car in a dirt parking lot adjacent to the building and warily eyed my surroundings. The building was small, consisting of pale stucco walls topped by the traditional Spanish tile roof. Despite my misgivings, I was encouraged by the fact that the parking lot was nearly full, and I decided to withhold judgment about the place until I got inside.

As I approached the place, I was greeted by the festive sounds of traditional Mexican music and the delightful aroma of cooked beef, pork, and chicken coupled with a variety of exotic odors that wafted from the entrance. My olfactory senses went on high alert when I opened the heavy wooden door and entered the dimly-lit interior. I was greeted by a pretty, Hispanic woman wearing a white peasant blouse and a colorful skirt.

"May I help you?" she asked in heavily-accented English.

Before I could answer, a strong hand gripped my arm and pulled me aside. I turned to see Ray Montijo standing beside me, offering me a bottle of Mexican beer and guiding me to a booth in the rear of the room. Alex was already there, sipping on what I suspected was a frozen margarita. It looked quite tasty, but I had my mind set on a beer, and the one Ray handed me was cold and refreshing.

I sat down and took a long sip of beer, while Ray slipped in beside Alex. The place was crowded and conversation was lively against the background of the traditional Mexican music. The smell of the food being served around us made my stomach growl and I remembered that I had skipped lunch.

Ray reached for a bowl of tortilla chips, took one, and dipped it in a small bowl of sauce. He popped it into his mouth and smacked his lips, "Very tasty," he said with a wide grin. Then he took a long sip of beer and signed with satisfaction.

I followed his lead, but seconds later I gasped for breath and quickly reached for my beer to extinguish the fire in my throat. Ray and Alex both laughed and I knew that I'd been set up.

"That's a bit hot for my taste," I gasped. "Do you have anything a bit milder?"

Alex laughed and pushed another bowl of sauce toward me and I tried it. I wouldn't call it mild, but I could tolerate it, and helped myself to a handful of chips.

"So, what's up, boss?" Ray asked, smiling broadly at my discomfort, while tipping his own bottle of Corona to his lips.

"I'm starved," I replied. "Can we order first?"

Ray said, "Not to worry, amigo, it's all been taken care of." He gave Alex a quick wink. She grinned, then took another sip from her Margarita.

I didn't know what was in store for me, but I practically grew up on Mexican food as a result of my Southern California upbringing, so I figured anything he ordered would be fine, and I wasn't disappointed.

A pretty young waitress who could have been the twin sister of the hostess arrived. Ray ordered another round of drinks and I quickly finished mine. Once we were alone, I began filling them in on the day's events. By the time I'd finished, our food had arrived, so we put aside our conversation and got down to enjoying what turned out to be an exceptional meal. Delicious food, the companionship of Ray and Alex, and the alcohol combined to make it a relaxing experience and helped take my mind off the tragic news from home.

There was still plenty of good food left when I reached my capacity, so I wisely pushed away my plate and savored my third Mexican beer, which was just as tasty and refreshing as the first one.

I gave them a quick rundown on the events in Climax. Alex glanced at Ray, then asked, "So, you think the car bomb in Climax may be the work of Ortega?"

I nodded and said, "I'm almost sure of it. It's definitely his M.O. I'd be willing to bet that the explosion in L. A. was meant to make it look like Ortega was dead so the police wouldn't be concerned about him any further. The body found in that explosion was probably some homeless person they picked up off the streets who bore a passing resemblance to Ortega."

"Well, if that's the case, Clint," Alex said, "You may be next on his list."

"Yeah," observed Ray, "once he knows you're in Capitol City, he'll sure as hell try to get you while you're here."

They were probably right. While the real purpose of my visit had not been made public, my presence in Capitol City was no secret.

"You need to take a few precautions just to be on the safe side," Alex said.

Ray grunted his approval.

I couldn't argue with them. "What do you suggest?"

Alex offered, "You need to find someone in the police department you can trust – maybe the Chief, or possibly ..."

"Or maybe Captain Wilkins," I replied.

Both Ray and Alex looked at me with surprise. Then I told them about my conversation with Herb Jenkins.

"Well," said Alex, "if the tape was doctored, that might mean that Wilkins is being set up."

"My sentiments exactly," I chimed in.

"And is that somehow connected with our investigation?" Alex suggested.

"That's hard to say," I said, "but that could mean that Wilkins is exactly the right person I need to take into my confidence."

I could see that Alex wasn't convinced that was a good idea. She said, "Are you sure you can trust him?

Then Ray offered, "From what I hear on the street, he's a pretty straight-shooter – tough, no nonsense, you know."

"That's my impression as well," I replied. "Very business-like. But when I saw him earlier today and he brought up the news about Donna Sanders, I saw real compassion in his eyes. I could tell he was deeply affected by the news of her death."

Alex said, "So, then, if you think you can trust Captain Wilkins, why don't you reach out to him for assistance?"

"Such as what?" I asked. "We need to keep a tight lid on our investigation, even if Wilkins is clean."

"Yeah," Ray agreed, "I guess you're right, Clint, but ..."

"I'll give it some thought," I said finally. "If it looks like we need help, I'll consider taking Wilkins into my confidence – but only as a last resort."

Alex sighed. "Well, I did find out one thing for sure." My pulse quickened. "What's that?"

"Those classification codes that Wilkins told you had no files in them?"

"Yes, what about them?"

"They're exactly what Wilkins said they were. My guy cracked open their so-called security system and found that it wasn't all that secure. Apparently, what Wilkins told you was true. There's nothing of interest in those files."

My initial enthusiasm dimmed at this news. "Well, okay, then, that's another reason to believe that Wilkins can be trusted."

"So where does that leave us?" Alex asked.

"I'm not sure," I replied. "I've found absolutely nothing suspicious in the police records, but we need to keep digging until we find out what's really going on here. I smell smoke, and where there's smoke ..."

"You got fire." Ray finished.

Alex and Ray exchanged glances; then Alex said, "Ray and I talked it over and have a suggestion."

"What's that?"

"You need to vacate that motel, Clint. Someone knows you're there, and the next time they might just plant something more than listening devices."

"Yeah, man," Ray chimed in, "you need to get outta there, like pronto."

I started to protest, but Ray cut me off. "Not to worry, Client. We got you covered."

Alex told me that her cousin Emily owned a second Airbnb home in Capitol City. "She's been renting it to a college student who's on a sabbatical in Europe for three months. Em said she'd be happy to let you stay there for that time."

"Well, that's awfully nice of her," I said, "but I –"

Ray cut in. "It's either Emily's place or you talk to Wilkins about finding you a safe house.

They've got to have one or two of those in this city."

I thought about it, then said reluctantly, "I suppose you're right. Hopefully, it will just be for a few days."

"Then it's settled," Alex said triumphantly. "Why don't we go by the motel, gather up your things, and head over to Emily's place."

A young Hispanic busboy came to collect the remaining food and dishes, and seemed to linger longer than necessary, as if interested in the conversation. I was apprehensive about saying anything further while the young man was present. He collected everything then made a hasty exit.

Then Ray spoke up. "I too have something of interest." Alex and I looked at him expectantly.

"Felipe tells me that the investigation into Donna's death is ongoing, but they have determined that the brake lines on her car were cut, which is why there were no skid marks left on the highway."

That news jolted me like an electric shock. Alex and I exchanged startled glances, and I knew she was thinking the same thing.

"So, the accident was no accident," Alex said. Ray nodded solemnly. "You got that right."

"Well," I said, "she was on her way to meet with me and apparently had something to tell me that she couldn't discuss at the office."

"Looks like we still have a mystery on our hands," offered Ray. "Yes," I said.

"I'm afraid so." I turned to Ray and asked, "What about her notebook?"

He shook his head sadly. "No sign of a notebook, but they're still checking."

That was disappointing news, and my heart sank.

"But I may have something just as good," Ray offered. "Felipe says they got Donna's laptop and cell phone from the car. They turned them both over to the forensic guys to see if there was anything on them that could explain why someone would want her dead."

"That's welcome news," I said. "How can we find out what they discover?"

Ray finished his beer and answered with a broad grin, "Just so happens one of their lab guys owes me a big favor – one that I'd rather not discuss in mixed company."

Alex gave Ray a knowing smirk, but said nothing.

I said, "When do you think we might know something?"

"I told him to put a rush on it," Ray replied. "I'll call him first thing tomorrow and see what he's got."

"Excellent" I replied. "We'll get back together tomorrow and talk about it"

"You bet," he answered.

I asked Ray for the check. He winked and said, "It's taken care of." I thanked him and we headed for the parking lot. Alex and Ray climbed into Ray's car and followed me back to my hotel where I hurriedly packed my things and checked out, apologizing to the desk clerk for the abrupt departure.

Thirty minutes later I was ensconced in a comfortable two-story home that was both modern and well-equipped. It was located in a quiet neighborhood, an easy drive to downtown Capitol City.

Before leaving, Alex showed me how to work the security system and gave me the combination to reset it. She also pointed out that there were several security cameras mounted outside the house which were monitored by the same system. It looked like a solid operation, and I was impressed.

"It's state of the art," Alex commented, monitored at a central operations command center. The police department communications center is automatically alerted if there's a security breach."

I had to admit that the residence was a step up from the hotel – while small compared to most rental houses I'd seen, it had two bedrooms, a quaint living room, one and one-half baths, a kitchen with a fully-stocked refrigerator and a few modern appliances, including a dishwasher and microwave oven.

My new home away from home, I thought. All I needed now was to have Mary Alice at my side, but that wasn't going to happen anytime soon, so I pushed the thought from my mind.

After Ray and Alex left, I set the alarm system as instructed. I found a comfortable recliner in the bedroom and settled back to call Mary Alice. It was nearly 10:00 PM and I knew she'd be waiting to hear from me. She sounded slightly better than she had the last time we'd talked, but her depression was obvious. I felt guilty that I couldn't be there to comfort her, but I knew she understood my situation.

I asked, "How are you holding up?"

"Oh, okay, I guess," she said without much enthusiasm. I could feel the tension in her voice.

"I'm here with Edna – she's such a dear. And Bruce has been just great. They're like a couple of doting grandparents and won't let me out of their sight."

She laughed lightly, and I felt a bit better. I was happy that she was in good hands.

"You're not planning on going back to work anytime soon, are you?"

"Hardly," she replied. "The explosion caused a lot of damage to the kitchen, so it will be a while before the diner's back in business."

I was relieved to hear that. I wanted her to maintain a low profile for her personal safety. I knew she'd want to go back to work as soon as possible, so having the diner out of commission temporarily was fine with me.

We talked for a few minutes longer and she promised to stay with Edna and

Bruce for a while, and I breathed a bit easier. I promised I'd be back there just as soon as I could wrap up things in Capitol City. She didn't ask for details and I offered none. She knew very well that I couldn't discuss with her what we were doing. I also didn't tell her about my sudden change in lodging since it would only worry her to know the reason for the move, and she didn't need anything else to be concerned about.

"I hope you'll be home soon," she said.

"Soon." I promised, hoping I'd be able to keep my word.

After we disconnected, I called Bruce Johnson and asked him for a progress report.

"Not much new here, Clint. The DEA guys confirmed that the car bomb had all the earmarks of Ortega's work."

"I'm not surprised," I said. "And I'm told that the body found in the L. A. fire is not Ortega, so he is alive and on the loose."

"And that means trouble for you – and maybe for Mary Alice too." "No question about it, Bruce. That bomb was almost certainly intended for Mary Alice, so please just –"

Bruce cut me off. "Clint, you don't need to worry none about Mary Alice. We're keeping a close eye on that little lady."

I knew I could count on Bruce, and his promise was reassuring. Mary Alice was about as safe as I could hope for; but the sooner I finished with my work in Capitol City and got back to Climax, the better I'd like it.

After disconnecting, I made a mental note to ask Captain Wilkins to make an appointment for me to meet with Commander Lance Underwood at the Community Outreach Center. It might not contribute anything to our investigation, but it was an intriguing program, and I wanted to learn more about it from a man who appeared to be a rising star in the CCPD.

CHAPTER 17

The following morning, I arose early and stopped to have breakfast at a coffee shop down the street from the police station. I arrived at work to find Captain Wilkins already in his office. I had to admire his work habits and professional attitude; probably explained why Chief Ryan placed so much trust and confidence in him. *But I wondered why would anyone want to frame him? What was the motivation? And who would gain by making him appear to be a crook?* These questions were pertinent to our investigation and I was determined to find the answers to them.

I stopped by Wilkins' office to say hello and was greeted with his customary business-like manner, but I was no longer bothered by it. I'd learned there was nothing personal in it – it was simply his style. He asked for a progress report and I gave him a generalized version of what I'd accomplished, but was careful not to mention what we knew about the death of Donna Sanders, or the situation in Climax. I still wasn't sure I could trust him completely, and the fewer people who knew about our mission, the more secure we would be. I also failed to mention my move to new quarters. This was bound to raise questions that I didn't want to answer.

"What do you have planned today?" he asked.

"I was looking over the reports on your Community Outreach Program," I said. "Very impressive."

"Yes, it is," Wilkins agreed. "Are you interested in taking a close-up look?"

"If it could be arranged," I answered, "that would be great." Wilkins nodded. "Let me see what I can do."

He picked up his phone and punched in a series of numbers. Someone picked up and Wilkins told them who I was and what I'd requested. After a few seconds, an answer was received. Wilkins said "Thanks," then hung up.

"Commander Underwood will be expecting you at 10:00 AM. I'm sure he'll give you full access to whatever you need. He's got an office in one of the community storefront centers on East Sheridan Avenue. It's not a very good area," Wilkins said. "Let me get someone to drive you there."

"That's really not necessary," I said. But I could see that Wilkins had serious concerns about my safety, so I relented.

He made another call and informed me that my driver would be by to collect me shortly. I thanked him and returned to my own office. In just a few minutes a tall, well-built man with a dark tan and buzz cut knocked on my door and informed me that he'd be my driver. He had a strong command presence and I could tell by the way he carried himself and the steely glint in his eyes that he could handle himself in a tough situation. He was dressed in casual clothes, but a bulge under his shirt was evidence of a bulletproof vest, and he carried what I figured was a Glock Model 19 in a holster on his belt. My first impression of him was that he was "combat ready".

"Marines?" I asked.

He shook his head. "Navy SEALs, sir." The pride in his voice was obvious, and justifiably so.

He extended his hand and said, "Sheriff Harrison, I'm Joe Butler.

I've heard a lot about you, sir."

I accepted his handshake and was impressed with his powerful grip. "Look, Joe, I really appreciate what Captain Wilkins has asked you to do for me, but I'm not used to having a ... uh ..."

Joe's face creased into a wide grin. "Just think of me as your 'escort,' Sheriff Harrison, and I'll try to stay as inconspicuous as possible."

Joe's easy manner was refreshing, and I felt comfortable in his presence.

"Then I guess we're off to see Commander Underwood," I said.

I detected a slight hesitation when I mentioned Commander Underwood, but Joe said simply, "I'm ready when you are, Sheriff Harrison."

He led me to a rear elevator that took us to an underground garage where all of the city's police vehicles were kept. We made our way to a big, black and shiny SUV. It was obviously no ordinary police car. It was probably armor-plated, with bullet-proof windows, heavy-duty shocks and a very powerful drive train. Clearly a VIP car, and I felt a little embarrassed at having it assigned to me.

Once on the street, I started to give Joe the address, but he waved me off. "I know where it's located," he said this with a hint of sarcasm, but I ignored it. Maybe some bad blood between Butler and Underwood? I wondered. But that happens even in police departments. Certainly nothing for me to be concerned about.

We arrived at the location a few minutes before 10:00 AM. Joe let me out and told me he'd be parked nearby, and gave me a card with his cell number on it.

"Call me when you're ready to go and I'll pick you up right here."

I said I would and surveyed my surroundings. I was standing in front of a small storefront located in what had to be one of the poorer and more rundown neighborhoods of Capitol City. I guessed that the building had once housed some kind of small retail establishment, but it and its neighbors had declined greatly over the years. The awning above the entrance was tattered and might easily be torn off with a heavy wind. The paint on the front was badly chipped and peeling. The place just had the look of decay and deterioration that seemed to perfectly match the neighborhood. If the Capitol City Police Department intended that its Community Outreach Program be located in the heart of poverty and social despair, I couldn't imagine a more fitting spot.

A musty smell greeted me as I entered the building, but I was surprised to find a well-lit and attractively-decorated front office, complete with a desk, file cabinet, desktop computer, and a friendly, plump black woman who greeted me with a wide smile. The nameplate on her desk identified her as Amanda Oliver.

"You must be Sheriff Harrison," she said warmly.

I admitted that I was and she rose from her desk. "I'll let Commander Underwood know you're here. Can I get you some coffee or something else?"

"Coffee would be great," I said. "Black, please."

She poured coffee into a mug and handed it to me. I accepted it and was rewarded by strong and pleasing aroma, and it tasted delicious. Smiling at my reaction, she invited me to sit down, then walked down the hallway to a nearby office, knocked twice on the door, and entered. She reappeared moments later, followed by a tall, well-built African-American man. He looked like he could have played tight end for the Denver Broncos. He was neatly dressed in khaki-colored slacks, a white, short-sleeved shirt, and brown loafers. He extended his hand and introduced himself as "Lance, short for Lanson, Underwood." His grip was strong and friendly, and I was immediately struck by his personal warmth and professional bearing. My initial impression was that the Chief Ryan had made a wise choice in selecting this man to head up this innovative new program.

"Sheriff Harrison, welcome. I've heard so much about you! It's a pleasure to finally meet you."

The man reeked charisma and natural charm, and it was hard not to have a favorable opinion of him.

I smiled. "Thank you, Commander, and I go by Clint."

He smiled back. "Very well then, Clint. Now, what can I do for you?

"I'm interested in getting some firsthand information about the Community Outreach Program," I replied. "I've read everything in the files, but I was hoping to get a more in-depth account of what you do here, and what results you've obtained."

Lance grinned broadly. "I'll be happy to enlighten you, Clint. Please have a seat."

He looked at his watch. "Amanda will be out running a few errands, so we may have a few interruptions, but I'll be happy to tell you what you need to know."

He proceeded to fill me in. I was fascinated by what he had to say, and listened intently.

The Community Outreach Program, according to Lance, was a multifaceted, mufti-disciplined program consisting of several components. Each of these components was nontraditional in nature, and as I listened, I realized that it was a very different approach to what typically was referred to as "community policing". Indeed, the programs he described had very little to do with tractional policing concepts. However, one aspect of traditional policing efforts – that of crime prevention – seemed to underlie much of the philosophy of the Community Outreach Program.

The key elements of the program included some broad and ambitious efforts such as the prevention of drug abuse, the alleviation of poverty and homelessness, the eradication of street-level violence and gang activity, along with other efforts that are usually deemed to be beyond the purview of traditional policing efforts.

As he spoke, the phone in the outer office rang incessantly, Lance smiled and explained, "We receive many requests for assistance from various community members, each of whom is seeking our help with a variety of local problems, ranging from public urination to uncollected trash to illegal parking."

"It must keep you awfully busy," I offered.

He shrugged and said, "We do our best to help people when no one else seems to care."

It was an impressive operation, and I could see the satisfaction he derived from being a positive source of assistance in that community.

After 30 minutes, Underwood said, "Do you mind taking a walk?" "Not at all," I said, anxious to see his world.

He informed Amanda that we'd be gone for an hour or so. We left the building and headed down Meridian Street. As we walked, Lance nodded at and spoke to nearly everyone he saw.

Clearly, he was a known and respected personality in this neighborhood.

"I grew up not far from here, Clint," he said, gesturing down the street.

I wondered what it must have been like to grow up in such a squalid and impoverished neighborhood, but I said nothing.

"It hasn't changed much," he said. "It's still one of the lowest income areas in Capitol City. It has the highest rate of violent crime and unemployment. And it's in the middle of a territorial turf war between three major street gangs."

It was a depressing thought, and I realized how hard it must be for someone to survive in such pitiful circumstances. But Underwood had, which made him even more impressive.

As if reading my thoughts, he said, "It was tough growing up here. I never knew my dad, and my mom was a coke addict. She shared her bed with just about any man who'd help her keep high."

It was a startling admission, but he seemed to be at peace with the story.

There was nothing remotely similar between his upbringing and my own. I'd been raised in a good home with strict but loving parents who made every effort to keep their children headed in the right direction. Of course, like most kids, I hadn't appreciated their efforts until much later in life when I became a parent myself.

"It's hard for me to imagine the challenges you must have faced," I admitted.

"Yeah, well, no big surprise that I started out hanging out with the wrong crowd. It was only dumb luck that I didn't end up dead or in prison like a lot of the guys I hung with."

We passed a group of young boys playing stick ball in the street and Lance asked them to move the game to a nearby vacant lot. They gave him a few jeers and stared coldly at me, but moved off in the direction he'd asked.

Is there anyone in this neighborhood Lance doesn't know, or who doesn't know him? I wondered.

He motioned me into an old, rundown tavern that had seen better days. We were assaulted by the odor of alcohol and stale cigarette smoke. We walked past a half-filled bar and entered a back room where several old men sat playing cards. Lance spoke to them and they greeted him warmly.

We sat down at a rickety table and Lance asked, "Coffee, tea, or soda?"

I'd had my fill of coffee and asked for a bottle of water. He went to the bar and returned moments later with my water and a chilled bottle of root beer for himself.

"That's your drink of choice?" I asked jokingly.

"When I'm working, you bet," he replied. "When I'm on my own time, I have slightly different tastes."

We both laughed and I asked him, "So what happened that changed your life?"

He paused and stared at nothing in particular, then said, "I was thirteen, going on thirty, a real badass, knew it all, and headin' for hell in a hurry."

He sipped his root beer, savoring the taste, and continued, "Calvin was my best pal. We did everything together. A lot of it I'm not too proud of today."

His voice trailed off as he took a walk down memory lane. Then he went on, "There was this old man who lived over on Brownstone Avenue, not far from here," he said, seeming to relive the experience as he spoke. "Word on the street was that he was loaded and kept tons of money hidden in the old house. So, Calvin and me, we decided to sneak in and help ourselves to some easy cash."

He sipped his root beer slowly and I waited patiently for 'the rest of the story.

"Long story short – we got caught inside. Some neighbor must have seen us break in. Cops came and we both panicked. Calvin found this rusty old .45 – probably something left over from the war – that wasn't loaded, and probably wouldn't have fired if it were. I don't know what he was thinking. Anyway, this one cop told him to drop it, and when Calvin pointed that old revolver in their direction the cop shot him."

There was sadness in his eyes. I could tell that the tragic story still haunted him.

"They rushed Calvin to the ER, but he didn't make it. I was hauled off to Juvenile Hall and did three years."

I sensed it wasn't a story he enjoyed telling, but he wasn't' finished. "While I was in Juvie, I met a man who helped me turn my life around."

"Who was that?"

"Father Greg Gallagher," Lance replied reverently. "He was one of the counselors assigned to Juvie. He took to me right away – I don't know why. He must've seen something worth saving. He started me going to church for the first time in my life. At first it felt weird, but then I got – I don't know – this feeling inside me saying 'you need to do this for yourself,' so I stayed with it. Later, Father Greg got me baptized and I received my first communion. That was a really big deal for me at that time."

Lance breathed deeply, then continued. "Father Greg was like a shepherd and I was the sheep. He got me to start taking high school classes. By the time I got out of Juvie, I had my GED, but he didn't stop there."

He took another deep breath, sipped again from his root beer and continued as the tenor of his story changed from sadness to pride. "Father Greg pushed me hard and wouldn't let me give up. He helped me get into community college, and then on to the university where I eventually received my Bachelor's and Master's Degrees. I owe everything I have to Father Greg."

"That's quite story," I said. "But you know, you must take some credit yourself for what you've accomplished. Which is a lot."

Lance nodded, but said nothing.

"Is Father Greg involved in the Community Outreach Program?" "No," he replied softly.

"Sadly, Father Greg passed away three years ago – way too soon. But I guess God must have had another mission for him, so He called him home."

The tenderness Lance felt for Father Greg was obvious, and I understood why. "I can see now how you can relate to some of the folks around here. You've walked in their shoes, and shared some of their experiences."

"Yeah, I have," he replied solemnly. "I feel their pain and try to share with them some of the hope I've found along the way."

We finished our drinks and left the tavern to continue our tour of the area, which I learned was known locally as "Old Town". Lance greeted people along the way and filled me in on the history of the area. His passion for the people and the neighborhood was obvious. He was truly a great representative of the police department, and I could see how he was ideally suited to head up the Community Outreach Program.

We walked by a small neighborhood park where a group of young children were playing noisily. He gestured toward an old bench near a scrubby-looking ball field, and we sat for a while, enjoying the warm sun and cool breeze.

"You know, Clint, here in the inner city, drugs, violence, poverty, unemployment and illiteracy are all tied together like some kind of crazy quilt. You simply cannot make headway in any of those areas without addressing the others simultaneously."

I nodded. Over my law enforcement career, I'd seen the same sorry story play out more times than I could count.

"So," he said proudly, "that's where our New Beginnings House comes in."

I hadn't come across this program during my research, so I asked him to tell me about it.

Underwood rose and said, "Come on, Clint. Let's take a look."

I followed him to a tired-looking three-story building that, like most of its neighbors, had seen better days, perhaps as a hotel? A crudely-lettered sign above the door announced it as the "New Beginnings House".

Lance ushered me inside and I was surprised to find a bright, modern interior. The furniture was inexpensive but attractive, and the clean white walls were tastefully decorated with paintings and lively-colored posters and photos. The place had a homey, comfortable atmosphere.

Lance introduced me to a smiling young Oriental woman named Rose Lee, who was smartly-attired in a colorful skirt and white short-sleeved blouse. Her makeup was modestly applied and she wore gold earrings and a matching gold bracelet.

"Very nice to meet you, Sheriff Harrison," she said. "May I offer you something to drink?"

I declined gratefully and Lance led me into an inner office where he introduced me to a young Hispanic woman who was just as nicely dressed as Ms. Lee. Her name was Esther.

"Welcome to New Beginnings, Sheriff Harrison. We don't get many visitors here. It's always nice to have the opportunity to show others what we do here."

"I'm all ears," I said, and she went on to tell me about the various things they did in that building. Meanwhile, Commander Underwood stood by, smiling broadly.

"Here at New Beginnings we try to offer the young people of our community just what the title says – new beginnings. A chance to get a fresh start, to undo past wrongs and to make something of themselves."

It sounded great, but I wanted to learn more.

"Working with our partners in other social service and criminal justice agencies," Esther continued, "we deal with some of the most disadvantaged young men and woman of our community. Many of these kids have no parents, no homes, and no real chance to enjoy a life without crime, drugs, poverty, and unemployment."

Lance cut in and said, "These kids get a fresh start here – regardless of what got them here. They get a place to sleep, three meals a day, and job training that will enable them to develop the skills they will need in their adult life."

"It sounds great," I said, "but it also sounds expensive. What's the source of your funding?"

Lance was ready with the answer. "The bulk of our funding comes from private donations, but we also get a few state and federal grants, and a small amount from some of our own fundraising activities, such as the Community Festival we put on once a year, pancake breakfasts, car washes, and anything else that comes to mind. The kids here work hard to make the program a success, and I'm proud to say that our overall success rate is very high."

Esther smiled broadly. "It's actually just over seventy-five percent to date."

I asked, "And how do you define 'success'?"

"Our definition of success," Esther answered, "is someone who has not reentered into a life of crime. Who is drug and alcohol free. And who has a regular job, regardless of how menial or low-paying. To many of these kids, who've never earned an honest dime in their lives, making ten bucks an hour at a car wash or busing tables in a mom-and-pop eatery, is success."

She said this with such enthusiasm that it was hard not to share it. "Very impressive," I said with admiration. "It's not every day you hear about a program of this kind that shows such achievement."

Lance went to a file cabinet and rummaged through several files, then pulled out a manila folder and handed it to me. "This is our most recent quarterly report. It should tell you everything you need to know about this program."

I accepted it, thanked him, and promised to review it. Then I looked at my watch and realized it was almost noon. "This is all quite admirable, but I think I've taken enough of your time. I'd better let you get back to work."

Lance and I thanked Esther and left for the Community Outreach Program office. On the way, we engaged in small talk, but my mind was on everything I'd learned in the last two hours. I was looking forward to reading the report Underwood had given me.

We arrived at his office and I thanked him. "It all seems like a great effort. You should be proud of what you've accomplished."

"It's really a team effort," Lance said modestly. "And it's had a remarkable impact on some of the quality-of-life issues here in the inner city. For example, illegal drug sales are down by thirty percent, and we now have the third lowest rate of homicide and person-on-person crimes in the city. We used to lead the rest of the city in both of these categories.

"I suppose," he continued, "it's hard for those who've not experienced it firsthand to understand how all these social ills breed the conditions that spawn crime. We've tried to address the root causes, and the results speak for themselves."

I nodded. I'd seen enough on the streets of L.A. to have a real appreciation for what this innovative program was trying to accomplish.

I thanked Lance and called Joe Butler, who pulled to the curb a few minutes later.

"Where to?" he asked.

"Back to headquarters," I replied, "but can we stop somewhere along the way? I'd like to pick up a sandwich and a soda."

"You bet," he said. "I know just the place."

Joe did, in fact, know just the right place. In short order, I was back in my office at CCPD enjoying a very tasty barbeque beef sandwich; crisp, golden-brown fries, and my own bottle of root beer. While I ate, I studied the reports Lance had given me and continued to be impressed by the early success of the New Beginnings Program.

CHAPTER 18

While Clint enjoyed his sandwich, a refrigerator-size man with dark hair, bushy black eyebrows, and a large nose sat on a wooden chair in a small room and called a number on his cell phone. It rang twice before being answered. "Yes?"

In a deep, baritone voice, the big man growled, "This guy Harrison could be a problem. I don't like it."

The other man replied calmly, "There's nothing to worry about, Frankie. We've got the situation under control."

Frankie fidgeted nervously. "I don't know, boss. I think Harrison may be gettin' too close. Maybe he should have some kinda accident, like –"

Boss cut him off, "Just relax and leave Harrison to me. I'll take care of him."

"Yeah, well maybe, but ..." Frankie said. "But what?" Boss asked sharply.

"There may be another problem."

Boss digested this information. "Another problem? Like what?"

Frankie hesitated, then said, "Harrison may not be working alone."

"What do you mean?"

"I got word that Harrison was spotted out at this Mexican restaurant having dinner with these two people – some Mexican guy and a good-lookin' babe."

"You sure it was Harrison?"

"No question about it. Harrison was all over the news last year when he busted up that illegal mining operation on the Indian reservation down in Climax," Frankie explained. "He's got a rep in that part of the state."

"Go on," Boss said, his voice showing piqued interest.

"Well, the guy who tipped me off works there clearin' tables. He says he's pretty sure he knows the guy who was with Harrison. He used to work undercover for the state drug task force. He saw him in court once and swears it's the same dude."

This definitely changed things, Boss realized. He said, "And what about the woman? Any idea who she is?"

"That I don't know," Frankie said, "but my guy said they looked like they were talkin' business, real serious-like. Not just out for social stuff."

"Any idea what they were talking about?"

"Nope. They clammed up when he came to clear off the dishes."

"So," Boss replied, "we can assume that Mr. Harrison may be working with these two – whoever they are." He paused, then said, "This does change the dynamics a bit, no question about it."

Frankie grunted, but had nothing else to offer.

After several seconds, Boss said, "Harrison is problem number one. If he goes away, the other two – whoever they are – can be dealt with much easier."

"That makes sense, I guess," Frankie said. "So, what's our next move?"

"It's very simple," Boss answered. "Harrison needs to be eliminated ... but it has to look like an accident. Can you arrange that?"

A broad smile broke over Frankie's face, and his pulse quickened. "I can certainly do that."

"Remember," Boss said, "it must look like an accident. We need this thing to go away without raising any suspicion. Otherwise, our whole operation could be in jeopardy."

"You got it, Boss. But what about the other two? They could mean trouble too," Frankie asked hopefully.

"Leave them to me," Boss replied. "You just take care of Harrison. I'll do the rest."

Frankie acknowledged, then disconnected and started making plans. As he thought about the assignment he'd just been given, a thrill of anticipation welled up inside him as it always did when his special set of skills were called upon. The nosey Sheriff Harrison was about to get what he deserved. This was the kind of action Frankie craved, and he was very good at it. He considered a number of possibilities, and savored the eventual outcome. He liked to think of himself as a good problem-solver, and this was the kind of problem that gave him the greatest sense of fulfillment.

Frankie rose and went to a small refrigerator. He took out a bottle of beer, snapped off the cap, and turned on the television set. In a few minutes, his favorite TV show, NYPD Blues, world be on. But first, he needed to give some thought to the termination of Sheriff Clint Harrison.

CHAPTER 19

I finished my lunch and continued my review of the files Underwood had given me. The results of the Community Outreach Program in just two short years were remarkable. The success of the program was one that other units of government would do well to emulate.

I was most impressed with the number of young people who had managed to find jobs. I'd learned, as a cop and a prosecutor, about the relationship between unemployment and crime. The ability to place young men and women from the inner city into honest jobs where they could earn both a decent wage and gain self-respect, could have a major impact on crime reduction. I was so intrigued at the program's claims of success that I decided to probe a bit deeper, but what I found – or rather, what I didn't find – sparked my curiosity.

Several of the reports contained startling claims about the number of young men and women who had been taken off the street, housed, fed, and educated, and for whom self-sustaining jobs had been found. But what was not in those reports – and which made me more curious – was a description of the type of jobs that these young people had secured. I wondered about this, and probed deeper into the reports, but without success. In addition, I saw nothing about the personal histories of these young men and women. The reports lacked information about where they came from, their family history, or their home life. I thought this information would be significant and I wondered why it was not included. Perhaps Underwood could clear all this up for me.

Knowing what type of employment had been found for these young people might be the key to really evaluating the success of the program. If most of the jobs turned out to be low-level and low-paying jobs with little or no hope of advancement, the true value of the program would be questionable. On the other hand, if these were well-paying jobs with good potential for career advancement, there was no question about the program's success.

Since I was unable to find the information, I needed in any of the reports Underwood had given me, I decided to see if I could find what I was looking for another way. I booted up the computer and logged in, then consulted the file directory. I began navigating through the multitude of files until I found the statistical reports dealing with the Community Outreach Program. Most of what I was seeing simply mirrored what I'd found in the files Underwood had given me. But the computer files did offer a bit more detail, and my spirits lifted in hopes of finding what I was looking for.

I finally discovered a table that looked like it might contain the information I was seeking. There were several column headings, including the applicant's name, the date of their inception into the program, the type of training received, and a final column labeled "placement". This last column seemed to be what I was looking for, but it contained nothing more than a series of five-digit numbers. These numbers, I supposed, were some sort of occupational classification. But without knowing what the codes represented, I was no further along than before, and my sense of frustration mounted. I placed a call to Underwood, but was informed he was not available, so I left a voicemail message asking him to call me.

Just then, there was a tap on my door and Captain Wilkins came in. He closed the door behind him and said, "Do you have a few minutes?"

"Sure." I gestured for him to sit down. He seemed a bit on edge and I wondered what he had on his mind.

"I'm concerned about your safety," he said with some urgency. His statement caught me off guard. "Why is that?"

"Let's just say that I have a reliable source that leads me to believe your safety may be in jeopardy."

"Can you be more specific?"

He shook his head. "No, I cannot. But I urge you to take my warning seriously."

I took a deep breath. "Okay. What do you propose?"

This seemed to relieve him. "I know about your moving to a new location. I'm good with that. I would have suggested it myself, but you moved before I could discuss it with you."

I wondered how he knew about my recent move, but he obviously had good resources, which was no surprise.

"Is there anything else you can suggest?"

"I'd like to have Joe Butler drive for you as long as you're here."

I wasn't sure I liked that idea. Could Wilkins be using Butler to keep an eye on me?

I thought about it, then said, "I really appreciate your concern, Captain Wilkins, but I don't believe it's necessary to assigned me a driver."

He apparently decided not to push it. He rose to go, then said, "Let me know if you change your mind."

I assured him I would, but figured there was not much chance of that. He left and I sat for a while, thinking about his warning.

I glanced at my watch and realized that it was nearly five o'clock. I decided to keep looking for what I needed later that evening. I pressed the PRINT icon and watched as several pages of the table in question quickly shot out from the printer. I switched off the computer, grabbed my briefcase, and headed for the police garage to collect my car.

I arrived back at my new "home away from home" and dialed Alex. She answered on the first ring. "What's up?"

"I need your help on something I found in one of the files I was checking earlier today."

"What that?"

I explained what I'd been doing all afternoon and briefed her on those unknown classification codes I'd come across. "They're all five-digit numbers, such as 15545, 15547, 15548, like that. I need to know what type of occupations they refer to."

"Okay," she replied, "but I'll need to look at what you have in order know how to track down the information you're interested in."

"I have several pages of files with me. Can I scan them and send them to you?"

"That works," she said. "I'll look them over and get back to you just as soon as I have an idea what they all mean."

"Great," I said. "Maybe those codes will tell a story." Minutes later, the files were on their way to Alex.

I called Ray and brought him up to date on my trip to see Lance Underwood. Then I asked, "Did the lab come up with anything useful?"

"Possibly," he replied. "What could that mean?"

"Well, they did find Donna's notebook."

I perked up. "That's great. Tell me more."

"That's just it, Clint. Most of what's in it seems like a bunch of gibberish, unless it's some kinda code."

"A code? Like what?"

"Well," he replied, "it's actually just a bunch of weird names." "Like what?"

"Well, let's see. How about names like Little Lolita, Baby Jane, and Cute Kid? Do those mean anything to you?"

"Not a thing," I replied. "What do you make of it?"

"Don't know, Clint, but I've got a guy at the state crime lab who works with all kinds of fancy software, one of which is supposed to be able to track and match millions of different name combinations. I asked him to check these out for us. He'll let me know if he comes up with anything."

"Good deal," I said. "Anything else?"

"I talked to one of the guys I know at the State Bureau of Investigation. He works cyber-crimes and is very good at it."

"What did he have to say?"

Ray paused, sighed, then said, "Well, it appears that your friend Donna may have been into some very kinky stuff."

His words jolted me and I didn't know what to say.

"Harry is pretty sharp, and he was able to crack into a couple of so-called Dark Web sites that Donna seemed to be interested in."

"I'm listening."

"From what Harry told me," Ray continued, "a lot of those Dark Web sites she had tried to access had to do with child porn and child prostitution, featuring very young children."

This news stunned me. It simply didn't jive with what I knew about Donna. Why would Donna be interested in anything so sordid? Then something Ray said clicked.

"Wait a minute," I said. "You said she had 'tried' to access those sites. Does that mean she didn't actually get into them?"

"I guess not," Ray replied. "Harry says the folks who create those websites have a lot of well-designed firewalls to keep the casual explorer – as well as law enforcement – from getting into them. There's no evidence that she was actually able to access them. But still... Do you think this may have something to do with her death?"

"Hard to say," I replied, "but I don't believe in coincidences."

"Me neither," Ray said, "but it doesn't give us much to go on."

No, it doesn't. But stay on top of this, Ray, and let me know the minute you learn anything else. Meanwhile, call Alex and bring her up to date on what you've learned."

He assured me that he'd stay in touch and we disconnected. I was still trying to digest what I'd just learned when my cell phone chimed. It was Alex.

"That was quick," I remarked. "What did you come up with?"

She hesitated momentarily, then said, "I'm not sure how helpful this will be, but it's sure beginning to get interesting."

"Please explain."

"Well, first of all," she replied, "the codes you sent me were not all that hard to decipher."

"Well, I guess that's good," I said, "but what do they mean?"

"They are U. S. Department of Labor classifications that are used to track national employment and unemployment trends. The D.O.L. classifications are actually eight-digit numbers, but the last five digits are the important ones. They relate to several hundred job classifications maintained by the Labor Department."

"And ..." I prompted her.

"And it appears that most of the codes fall into a category called 'domestic services.'"

"Domestic services?" I echoed.

"Yes. It turns out that 'domestic services' is sort of a catchall category for maids, housekeepers, gardeners, chauffeurs ... and things like that. Another one is for physical therapist."

"Physical therapist? That seems rather odd."

"I thought so too," she agreed, "and when you match this information with the age and gender of those who were employed, it sets off alarm signals in my mind."

"Such as what?"

"Such as the fact that most of those people who were hired into those so-called 'domestic service' occasions, were mostly teenagers – some as young as thirteen."

This information was alarming. "Can there be a logical explanation?"

"Not that I can think of," she said, "I checked and double-checked the figures to make sure they're correct."

I thought about it for a moment. "If I didn't know better, I'd say we're dealing with some sort of slave trade. But that's just not possible unless ..." I was sickened by what I was thinking and I wondered if she had reached the same conclusion."

"There's something else you need to know, Clint." The tone of her voice alarmed me.

"What's that?"

"I spoke with a friend of mine who works for the local organized crime task force. He told me this in strict confidence, but I said I had to share it with you. He agreed, as long as it goes no further."

"Go on."

"Well, it seems that the task force is looking into Donna's death."

"That's odd," I said. "Why would they be interested in her death, unless ..."

"Unless," Alex echoed, "Donna had information about something they were working on. Like maybe what she had in that little notebook. Or, unless Donna was not who you think she was."

That suggestion came right out of left field. "What do you mean?"

Alex took a deep breath. "Is it possible that Donna was working for another agency? Maybe in some kind of undercover capacity?"

That thought hadn't occurred to me, but Alex could be onto something.

"I suppose that's possible," I admitted. "But who could that be – and why?"

"Maybe what she was doing is what got her killed," Alex replied.

"Possibly," I said. "Any chance you can find out what it was?"

"I'm not sure, but I'll try," she said. "These guys can be very tight-lipped."

"Do your best." I sighed. "It's possible that whatever Donna was involved in may be connected with our own investigation."

"I'll let you know the minute I learn something," she said. "In the meantime, where do we go from here?"

"I'm not sure," I said. "I need think on it. Maybe a good night's sleep will help me get it all sorted out."

"I'm good with that."

"Let's plan on getting our heads together tomorrow and do a little brain-storming. I'll give you both a call and we'll decide when and where."

"Sounds like a plan," she said, and disconnected.

It was getting late, but I suspected I wasn't going to get much sleep that night. I needed something to take my mind off the events of the day. I took a beer from the refrigerator, went upstairs to the bedroom, and settled into a comfortable recliner. I found a John Grisham novel on a bedside table and managed to get through three chapter before falling into an uneasy sleep. But my slumber was rudely interrupted a short time later.

CHAPTER 20

I awoke with a start, sensing danger, but unaware of just what it was, and struggled to clear the cobwebs from my mind. I felt woozy and found it difficult to focus on my surroundings. Through the haze that clouded my mind, I recognized the odor of natural gas, and went on full alert.

I jumped out of the recliner, sending the novel flying, then stumbled into the hallway, only to discover that the odor was even stronger below me. I retreated into the bedroom and made my way to the window, desperately seeking fresh air. But the window was stuck tight and I was unable to force it open. Aware that I might have only seconds to act, I looked desperately for something I could use to break the window. I settled on the bedside table.

I fought off the overpowering effect of the gas, summoned all the strength I could muster, and heaved the small table though the bedroom window, then fell to the floor, exhausted. Cool air rushed through the shattered window. I breathed deeply, trying to clear my lungs of the noxious fumes.

The blast came without warning, accompanied by a thunderous noise and a concussive force that shook the entire house as if it had been struck by a tornado. In seconds, the odor of gas was replaced by dark, choking smoke, intense heat, and the sound of walls collapsing below me. A glance at the hallway told me that the entire first floor was engulfed in flames. The only possible way to escape was through the shattered bedroom window. I could feel the searing heat as it drew nearer. The raging flames would soon reach the second floor.

I placed my handkerchief over my face to keep from breathing the oppressive smoke and made my way to the broken window. My only chance for survival was to drop two floors to the ground below. It was risky, but I was running out of time.

I crawled through the window to get a better view of my situation, being careful not to cut my hands on small shards of broken glass. It was a good 20-foot drop to the ground below, and the chances of my landing without severely injuring myself were slim or none. But the blaze had now reached the second floor and time was running out.

I spotted a giant oak tree about five feet from the window. If I could jump and grab hold of one of the nearby branches, I might be able to climb safely down to the ground below. It was a gamble, but it seemed the best option.

The plan was workable, but the execution was poor. As I launched myself from the window, I grabbed the closest branch, but it wasn't strong enough to support my weight. I heard a loud crack and desperately reached for another branch, but couldn't hold on, and I fell to the ground much quicker than I intended. The fall knocked the breath out of me and I cracked my head on a large tree root. Stars shot through my brain, and I was unable to focus. Wracked by pain, I lay there, watching helplessly while the house became totally engulfed in flame.

Suddenly, I was shocked to find myself being dragged roughly across the grass and away from the flames.

"You'll be a lot safer here," a woman's voice said.

I looked up to see a large African-American woman, who could have played linebacker for the Los Angeles Rams, looking down at me. She probably tipped the scales at two fifty or better; but she had kind eyes and a warm smile that helped me forget the pain I was in.

"I'm Pearl, from over there," she said, gesturing toward the house next door. "And that's Sampson." She pointed to a massive St. Bernard who was licking my face with his very large and very wet tongue.

"Thanks, Pearl," I said, gently pushing Sampson away and offering my hand instead.

"Thanks for your help. I'm Clint Harrison and I'm –"

I was interrupted by wailing sirens announcing the arrival of a fire engine, followed by two more. Seconds later, firefighters clad in turnout gear and carrying hose lines began to attack the fire. More sirens signaled the approach of additional fire and rescue vehicles.

I struggled to sit up and take stock of my surroundings. I realized that Pearl may have saved my life, as the spot where I had fallen was now covered with burning debris and smoldering embers. Despite the efforts of more than a dozen firefighters, who were now attempting to keep the flames from spreading to adjacent structures, the building in which I'd been sleeping just moments earlier was now fully involved. I shuddered involuntarily as I realized how close I had just come to dying in the raging fire.

"You took a nasty fall," Pearl said, reminding me of the pain that continued to wrack my body.

"I'm lucky you came along when you did," I said, trying to get to my feet.

"You'd best lay still, son," Pearl said, and gently pushed me back to a sitting position. "Let's let the paramedics take a look at you. They'll be here any minute."

I did as she said, then asked her how she came to be there when I fell.

"Darn lucky I'd say," she answered. "I heard Sampson making a ruckus at the front door. Soon's I got up I could see the flames next door, so I called 911. Then I rushed outside just in time to see you fall from that tree. For a minute I thought my mind was playing tricks on me. Then I realized I'd better hurry up and get you away from there."

I was still woozy when the paramedics arrived and rushed to my side. Pearl gave them a shorthand version of what had happened while they checked my vital signs and asked me the usual questions. In the meantime, the fire crews were still working to get the fire under control, but there wasn't much left of the house except charred rubble. I felt bad about Alex's cousin, and hoped she had good insurance.

While the paramedics worked on me, I was surprised to see Joe Butler arrive. "What the hell happened here, Sheriff?" he asked in amazement.

My first response was a bad attempt at humor. "Isn't this a bit past your bedtime, Joe?"

He chuckled. "I monitor emergency calls on my scanner at home.

When I heard the address, I hurried over. So, what happened?"

"It was a gas explosion, I think. I tried to get out through an upstairs window, but took a bit of a fall."

I nodded to the neighbor and said, "Pearl here managed to pull me to safety."

Joe glanced at Pearl, then looked back at me. "It's a wonder you weren't killed."

For the first time, it occurred to me, Maybe that's what someone had in mind? But I kept that thought to myself.

I noticed that Sampson was staring at Butler and growling softly. Butler stepped back, seeming fearful of the large dog. Pearl called Sampson to her and he sat obediently at her side, but his attention was still fixed on Butler.

Pearl excused herself saying, "Well dearie, I can see you're in good hands, so I'd best get back to my place." She placed a friendly hand on my shoulder. "You take care of yourself, Mr. Harrison."

I promised her I would and thanked her for what she'd done. But my words seemed totally inadequate for the debt I owed her. She waved and headed home with Samson trailing along at her side.

The paramedics finished their examination and told me that there were no broken bones, but that they recommended I get checked out by a doctor, just in case. I nodded, but I had no intention of doing so. My body ached like hell and I'd probably have a few bruises to remind me of the night's events. But there was nothing wrong with me that time wouldn't heal.

After the paramedics left, Joe helped me to my feet and I followed him to his car. "If you're sure you don't need medical attention, I'll take you to some place where you can rest up."

We got into his car and sped away; destination unknown.

"Don't worry about your personal effects," Joe said. "There will be plenty for you where we're going."

"Thanks, Joe," I replied. "I'm lucky you came along when you did."

Then I felt in my rear pocket and was relieved to find my cell phone where I'd put it the last time I'd used it. I was grateful to find that it still worked, in spite of the impact of the fall. Then I realized that I'd left my briefcase with my laptop in my car, which was still parked at Alex's cousin's place.

"Joe, I need to go back and retrieve few things from my car, if you don't mind."

He was happy to oblige me. Fortunately, I'd also left an overnight bag with a change of clothes in the trunk of my car. I'd parked it in a garage at the rear of Emily's house, safe from the fire that had destroyed the house.

We were soon on our way to a new "safe house". On the way there, I quietly gave thanks to God that I'd survived the ordeal. But once again, I wondered if the gas leak and explosion had been simply an accident, or something much more sinister. Was it possible that I was getting too close to the truth, and the fire was intended to get me out of the way, permanently?

We soon arrived at a small one-story residence located in a pleasant-looking neighborhood. It was not as roomy as my previous abode, but it was clean and had a somewhat complicated security system that Joe briefed me on. It was after two o'clock when Joe left, and I asked him to pick me up at 8:00 AM. I was both exhausted and unnerved by the ordeal, but I knew I had to let Alex and Ray know about my situation.

I called Alex and apologized for waking her up; then quickly summarized what had happened and told her my new location.

"Oh my God, Clint," Alex gasped. "Are you okay?"

"A little banged up, but, nothing serious," I assured her. "I'm afraid Emily's house is a total loss, though. I feel horrible about it. Especially if someone was gunning for me."

"Well, it's not your fault, Clint. You didn't cause the explosion. And I'm sure she has insurance. I'll call her tomorrow and give her the bad news. Are you sure you're okay?"

"Yes, I'm fine. Can you call Ray and let him know?"

"You bet. But are you sure this was an accident?"

"Actually, no I'm not. But we should know more after the arson investigators finish their work."

"Can I do anything? Other than calling Ray, I mean?"

"I don't think so. I'll sleep on it and reach out to you both later today and we'll see where we are."

She agreed and I disconnected. I was mentally and physically exhausted and fell into bed, hoping to get a few hours' sleep before Joe returned to pick me up. But something Joe had said was bothering me, and I couldn't put my finger on it. As I drifted off into a fitful sleep, I had a feeling that the pieces of this crazy puzzle were about to fall into place, but I didn't know how.

I woke at 7:00 AM, still feeling groggy and hurting. I showered, and got dressed, then tried to navigate the instructions for the one-cup coffee maker in the kitchen, but gave up in disgust. Just then Joe Butler knocked on the door. I opened it and he handed me a steaming cup of coffee and a bag containing a frosted cinnamon roll.

"Ahh ... Just what the doctor ordered – and low-cal too, I'll bet," I quipped.

Joe laughed and said, "Cops are all the same. A cup of joe and a donut is all they need to keep them happy."

He waited while I grabbed my phone and briefcase, then headed for his car. On the way, we stopped by Emily's place to retrieve my car. I gazed sadly at the ruins that had once been a house and said a silent prayer to St. Anthony for bringing Pearl to my rescue.

CHAPTER 21

I followed Joe to police headquarters, and in a few minutes I was in my office. I was enjoying my coffee and roll when Captain Wilkins appeared at my door. The grimace on his face told me he wasn't happy. "What the hell happened last night?"

I briefed him on the night's events.

Wilkins shook his head in disbelief. "I should have insisted that you stay in one of our safe houses."

He was right, so there was no point in arguing about it.

"You move in one day and you have a gas explosion and fire in less than twenty-four hours? It doesn't pass the smell test."

"I'm thinking the same thing," I replied. "How about –"

Wilkins headed me off at the pass. "I've got our bomb and arson investigators heading there now."

"Good idea," I replied. "I'll be interested in what they find."

"You'll be the first to know," Wilkins replied. "In the meantime, I'm going to insist that Joe Butler take you wherever you need to go. Ultimately, we're responsible for your safety and we don't need any –"

"I get it," I said reluctantly, but I knew better than to argue. Besides, Joe was a fellow Marine, so what was not to like?

By this time, I'd made up my mind that Wilkins was someone I could trust, so I decided to take him into my confidence. I filled him in on Carlos Ortega, and suggested that he might be responsible for the explosion and fire.

Wilkins thought about this, then said, "Okay, then. Give me all you have on Ortega. I'll get the word out. If he shows up in Capitol City, we'll know it in short order."

"That may not help," I replied. "Ortega is too careful to get his hands dirty on this kind of thing. I'm sure he'd send one of his henchmen."

"I'll see if I can get a line on any of his crew or associates," Wilkins offered. "In the meantime, you stay close to Butler and try to keep a low profile. Did Joe check you out on the security system?"

"It appears to be very good," I said.

"State of the art," Wilkins said. "To bad you didn't have something like that last night."

"Actually," I replied, "that house did have a security system, but it must have failed somehow."

Wilkins frowned, "Are you sure you set the system property?" "Absolutely, I checked and double-checked it."

"And it never went off?"

"I assure you, it did not. Nor can I explain why."

Wilkins rose to leave. "That's certainly suspicious. I've never heard of one of those systems failing unless it was deliberately shut off or disconnected."

"I agree." I was relieved that Wilkins was thinking the same thing. After Wilkins left, I felt a bit more secure knowing that the word on Carlos Ortega and his henchmen would soon be out on the street. But I also knew the chances of catching him were slim. He was just too cagey.

I finished the cinnamon roll and coffee, then called Ray to see if he had anything to report.

He wasted no time in offering his own opinion of the night's events. "For Christ's sake, Clint, that don't sound like no accident!"

"I know, Ray," I said. "We don't know for sure if it was arson, but –"

"But still, Clint," Ray jumped in, "I don't like this at all. You coulda been killed. You think this could have somethin' to do with our investigation?"

I hesitated before answering. It was certainly possible that we were getting too close to what was going on in Capitol City. But it was also possible that the explosion and fire were the work of Ortega. Since I hadn't briefed either Alex or Ray on Ortega, I didn't want to mention that possibility. I wanted them to stay focused on our own investigation and not be distracted by Ortega.

"It's possible. And if so, it must mean we're making progress. That's a good thing," I said, trying to put a positive spin on the situation.

"I suppose," Ray growled, "but I still don't like it. Maybe we should come up with a better security plan?"

"I think we're okay," I insisted. "In the meantime, did the lab come up with anything else in Donna's notebook?"

"Not really," Ray said. "Still just a few odd words and phrases that no one can make heads or tails of."

"Like what?"

I could hear him riffling through some papers, then he said, "Like, for example, 'N.B., 538, 545, 558 ... jobs or ... followed by a question mark."

"That's not very helpful," I agreed. "Anything else?"

"Maybe one thing good," Ray offered. "They recovered Donna's cell phone from the crash. It's pretty beat up, but they're trying to see if they can recover some files she stored on the phone."

"What kind of files?"

"Don't know for sure, but they'll let me know what they find." "What about her phone records? Have they been checked out?"

"Yep," he replied, "but there was nothin' unusual."

Another possible lead gone dry. We needed something to get some momentum going in our investigation. I was growing impatient with our lack of progress.

"Let me know just as soon as you hear something." "You bet, Clint."

"I'll check in with Alex and see if she has anything. Well get together later today to compare notes."

Ray agreed and we disconnected. Seconds later, my cell phone chirped. It was Alex.

"Did Ray call you?" Alex blurted out. "He was awfully upset about what happened."

"Yes, I just spoke with him. I think I got him settled down a bit." "Good," she said.

"He can get a little tight when things get a bit crazy." She laughed and I laughed with her.

"So where are we, Clint?"

"Regrettably, nowhere new at this point," I said. "But we can't ignore the possibility that what happened last night was no accident."

"Then we need to re-double our efforts to find out what's going on behind the scenes. So, what do you suggest?"

"I'm not sure," I said. "Let's get together later today and do a little old-fashioned brainstorming. Maybe we can shake something loose."

"Sounds good. Where and when?"

"Your call," I replied. "You know the city better than I do."

She thought for a moment. "There's quiet little place not far from police headquarters. Can we meet there for lunch?"

"Away from prying eyes?"

"You bet," she said. "I know the owner and they have a very cozy back room we can use."

I looked at my watch and decided that would work. "Sounds like a plan. I'll have Joe Butler drop me off."

She gave me the address and we agreed to meet there at noon. She promised to pass this on to Ray and then disconnected.

My next call was to Lance Underwood.

"New Beginnings," said Amanda Oliver. "How may I help you?"

I told her it was me and asked to speak with Commander Underwood.

"Just a minute please, and I'll see if he's available."

I waited for sixty seconds or so before Amanda informed me that Commander Underwood was in a meeting, and asked if I would mind leaving a message. I did so, and told her that I only needed a minute of Underwood's time to ask him one or two quick questions. She politely assured me she'd give him the message and that I would hear back from him shortly.

I busied myself by reviewing some of the reports Underwood had given me the day before. In less than thirty minutes, my phone rang.

"Sheriff Harrison," Lance said. "It's good to hear from you again.

How may I assist you?"

"I just need a bit of clarification on some of the reports you provided me yesterday."

"Anything to help," he assured me.

When I told him that I was interested in getting a breakdown of the employment classifications in the reports, however, his tone changed.

"What exactly is it that you need to know?" he asked, his voice showing just a bit of – what? – irritation? I wasn't sure.

I went on to explain what appeared to be some contradiction in the types of employment being referred to in the reports, but I was careful not to suggest that I suspected anything other than a lack of understanding on my part.

My explanation was followed by an awkward period of silence, during which I got the distinct impression that I was venturing into forbidden territory. But why? When there was no response, I said, "Commander, what I mean is –"

"I understand your question, Sheriff Harrison. What I don't understand is the relevance of your inquiry. How is that at all related to your audit?"

Underwood's tone had turned hostile, and I suspected that he was trying to keep something from me. And his unusual response to my request only fueled my curiosity.

I tried to remain cordial. "I'm just trying to tie up a few loose ends. If it's too much bother I'll be happy to come to your office."

He seemed to regain his composure. "No need for that, Sheriff Harrison. It's just that we're in the middle of our annual performance evaluation here and things are a bit crazy. Can you give me a day to pull that information together?"

I assured him I could wait. He promised to get back to me in 24 hours. I thanked him and disconnected. I sat for a while, thinking about the conversation with Underwood and wondering what was so important in the information I'd asked for. There was no doubt in my mind that my request had startled Underwood and put him on the defensive.

CHAPTER 22

Ray rose just before dawn as he did each day. He wanted to get in a quick, two-mile jog, just in time to see the sun creep over the eastern horizon. He'd been initiated into this routine when he was in the U. S. Marines' elite Force Recon Division.

After his run, he showered and dressed, and thought about the events of the last 24 hours. He was about to check in with Alex when his cell phone chirped. His positive attitude changed abruptly when he looked at the caller ID: It was his ex ... Estelle.

"Hi, Estelle," he said, trying to remain buoyant. "What's up?" "What's up? You wanna know what's up?" She was angry, and he knew why.

"Look, Estelle," he cut in. "I know the check is a couple-a days late, but –"

"So, what's the excuse this time?" she yelled. "Is it another payroll problem? Or something went wrong at the bank?"

The anger in her voice cut him to the quick, and some of the reasons they were no longer together flashed through his mind. Regardless of how much he loved her, he just couldn't deal with her during the worst periods of her bipolar episodes. The meds she took only helped when she remembered to take them. And she wasn't always careful about taking them when she should.

"No, nothing like that," he said apologetically. "I was gonna bring the check to you so I could see Lilly, but I got tied up on a big case and I –"

"Yeah, well," she cut him off, "you're always on some big case, aren't you? Just like you always got an excuse for being late with the child support. Meanwhile, Lilly needs clothes for school and we have no food in the frig."

Her words stung like bee, and he knew she had every right to be angry. He had no excuse, and they both knew it.

"I screwed up, Estelle, and I'm sorry. Look, I'll drop off the check this morning, I promise. I'll head up to your place in just a few minutes."

His promise seemed to throttle down her anger, and she told him she'd be there until noon, but then she had to leave for work. He promised to be there well before that and she disconnected without another word. Ray was upset with himself and hoped the rest of the day would go better than it had started.

Alex had called him the evening before and let him know about their noon meeting. Which meant he needed to get moving to make it back in time. He skipped breakfast and left a few minutes later. He dreaded the drive to Estelle's place, but was anxious to see his daughter. She was seven years old and growing so fast and wouldn't be a little girl much longer. As he drove, all the old memories of his seven-year marriage to Estelle – the good ones and the bad ones – flashed back.

Lilly was definitely the best thing that had come from their union.

Almost from the beginning, their marriage had been a stormy one, filled with lots of love, great sex, and very tender moments. Those memories were counterbalanced against times of aggravation, frustration and anger. He knew he'd always love her, and he was pretty sure she felt the same way. Their divorce was inevitable, and they parted on more or less amicable terms.

Neither had found a suitable partner since their divorce five years ago, which might say something about their lingering affection for each other.

The birth of Lilly had been the highlight of their marriage. She was the glue that had held them together, but only on a very fragile basis. Estelle's erratic mood swings became increasingly hard for him to deal with, and his own failures had contributed to the breakup of their marriage as well. There was plenty of blame to go around. Now he had one more thing on his To Do list. And this one had top priority.

While on the road, he used his cell phone to access his savings account and transferred enough money to cover the payment to Estelle. He could have simply had the money electronically transferred to Estelle's account, but bringing her the check in person might help to make up for his failure in her eyes. And it would give him an excuse to see Lilly Being a part-time dad was one of the hardest things he'd ever experienced.

Ray stopped at a convenience store to get a large coffee, then headed north on Highway 19. The two-hour drive to Mesquite was scenic, but could also be treacherous owing to the sharp hairpin curves leading up though a steep maintain pass. It was only 90 miles as the crow flies, but the rugged terrain and winding road made the going slow. Ray settled back to enjoy the good weather, marvelous scenery, and the throbbing lyrics of Credence Clearwater blaring from his satellite radio.

Ray's reverie was interrupted when his cell phone chirped and jolted him back to reality. He glanced at the screen but didn't recognize the caller's number. "Montijo here."

"Ray, it's Loren Anderson," said a husky feminine voice. "Remember me?"

Ray searched his memory for the name, but came up with nothing. The woman said, "We worked that organized crime case together, last year, down in El Mirage County."

The image of a tall, slender, and good looking African-American woman with straight black hair, high cheek bones, ebony eyes, and a mischievous smile slowly emerged from the shadows of his memory.

"Loren! Hell yes," Ray said excitedly. "How are you?" He was a bit embarrassed at failing to recognize her immediately. She was a terrific undercover operator who worked for the state's Bureau of Criminal Investigation. Their success in putting several high-ranking members of a notorious organized crime ring behind bars was due largely to her hard work. And it had nearly cost Loren her life.

"Oh, you know Ray," she chuckled, "still putting scumbags behind bars, where they belong. How about you?"

"Well, I'm working a big case with Alex Arrowsmith. You remember her?"

"Oh yeah," she replied. "Real sharp gal."

"You bet," he said. "So, what can I do for you, Lorren?" He knew she wasn't calling to reminisce.

"I hear you're up in Capitol City working with this guy Harrison from down in Climax."

Ray was stunned. Their mission was supposed to be deep undercover. How could Loren – or anyone else – know about it? Had their cover been blown?

Before he could reply, she said, "It's okay, Ray. You should know that we have our sources. And don't worry! Your operation is well protected."

"Okay," Ray replied cautiously, "but then how –"

She cut him off, “Look Ray, I don’t have time to go into it now, but I may have information that will help your investigation. When can I meet with you and Harrison?”

Ray thought for a minute. He wondered if it’d be safe to bring her into a meeting with Alex and Clint unannounced; then decided it was probably not a good idea.

“Look, Loren,” he said, “I’ve got to clear this with Sheriff Harrison first. You understand.”

“Yeah, I do,” she replied, “but my info is hot. You need to move on it quicky. And Ray,” she paused for emphasis, “be very careful. These people – the ones you’re dealing with – play very, very rough, and they may already be on to you. So, watch your back!”

Her words were ominous, and he thought about the fire that had nearly cost Clint his life. He told her he’d get back to her as soon as he could talk with Sheriff Harrison. She accepted his promise and, before disconnecting, urged him once more to be careful.

Since they hadn’t gained much traction themselves, her offer was welcome news. He was anxious to bring it to Harrison’s attention. Ray was so deep in thought that he paid little attention when the large pickup truck with oversized tires pulled in behind him. But he became fully alert when the truck punched his rear bumper with a powerful thrust that Ray knew was no accident.

The coffee cup flew out of his hand and burned his arm as Ray tried desperately to regain control. But his small sedan was no match for the powerful truck. The F-350 raced up and struck Ray’s rear bumper again, this time forcing Ray to turn the wheel sharply to avoid the steep drop-off several feet to his right. Ray pressed the accelerator, trying desperately to put distance between himself and his pursuer. But he was seriously over-matched. There was no way he could outrun the powerful truck. He braced himself for yet another collision, hoping he'd be able to keep his car on the road until they reached a turnout, less than a mile ahead.

But Ray's luck had run out. The third impact, more powerful yet, sent Ray's car careening out of control. It veered crazily to the right, up and over the small retaining wall, and crashing down the side of the mountain in a shower of dirt, rocks and brush. Ray had no time to brace himself for the impact and instantly regretted his lifelong disdain for seat belts. Then, in a thunderous, bone-crushing crash, Ray's world disintegrated in a flashing light that dissolved into total darkness.

CHAPTER 23

Just before noon, Alex arrived at the small, nondescript restaurant, just a few blocks from police headquarters. She seated herself in a rear booth and informed the hostess that she would be joined by two associates. Ray was a stickler for punctuality, so she was surprised not to find him there on her arrival. She dialed his number on her cell and was again surprised when he didn't pick up. Instead, it went to his voicemail after several rings. She'd always been able to reach him by phone before, and a wave of uneasiness came over her. She then tried to call Clint, and got the same result. Her uneasiness grew into a full-out alarm. The fact that neither Ray nor Clint could be reached was a sure sign that something must be terribly wrong.

A pretty young waitress approached and Alex ordered coffee, indicating that she would wait to order something to eat until her two companions arrived. But the feeling of dread she was experiencing told her she wouldn't be ordering anything further. The waitress returned promptly, filled Alex's cup with steaming, aromatic coffee, and left the pot on the table. The coffee was delicious, but did nothing to settle Alex's nerves that were by now taut as violin strings.

Alex decided to try to track Ray using her cell phone's GPS tracking device, but when she punched in his number, she became even more concerned. The readout indicated that Ray was at a point well north of Capitol City – a very desolate and mountainous area. She could think of no legitimate reason why Ray would be in such an area. And wouldn't he call her if he was running late? It simply didn't make sense. The sinking feeling in the pit of her stomach became more intense. She did her best to maintain her composure, and tried Harrison's number again, but got the same result. She used her tracking device in an attempt to learn Harrison's position, but oddly the signal appeared to be disabled. She considered that her inability to reach either of them could mean they were both in trouble. As she waited, a troubling sense of foreboding descended on her.

Her coffee forgotten, Alex knew that she needed to act quickly. She consulted her phone's contact list, then dialed a number. After three rings, a man's voice answered. "Yeah ... who's this?"

"It's Felix, Alex."

Felix Morales, a captain with the state police, was in charge of the agency's drone fleet.

There was no response for several seconds, then the man said, "Oh, hey, Alex, how the hell are you? And what – "

Alex cut him off, "Felix, I need your help and it can't wait." Felix perked up. "Well, sure, Alex, what is it?"

"Felix, you're still in charge of the State Police's drone fleet, right?" "Why, sure, Alex. We've got a dozen drones available for action. Why?"

"Listen, Felix, I don't have time to explain, but I need your help in locating someone. It's urgent."

"Well, okay, Alex. What do you have?"

"If I give you the coordinates, how quick can you get one of those birds up in the air?"

He thought for a moment, then said, "Well, of course, that all depends on where."

"It's close by, I think. Probably a fifty-mile radius from your base." "Well, hell then Alex," he responded, "that shouldn't take long at all. Give me those numbers."

She consulted the tracking device on her cell phone and gave him the coordinates. While she waited, he punched keys on a keyboard. She could hear him whistling to himself while she mentally crossed her fingers.

After what seemed like forever, but was probably no more than a minute or two, Felix said, "Okay. The bird's in the air. What am I looking for?"

Alex gave Felix a description of Ray's car and waited with nervous anticipation as she listened to Felix tapping the keys of his keypad.

Several more minutes passed before Felix said, "Uh-oh, I think I have something and it doesn't look good."

Alex's heart pounded. "Why? What is it?"

"I see what appears to be the car you described at the bottom of a steep cliff. It's smashed up pretty bad. I'm trying to get a closer look to see."

"Oh my God," Alex cried, crossing herself. "Please, God, tell me that he's not –"

This time it was Felix who interrupted. "I see a man's body. Looks like he may have been thrown clear from the crash."

Before Alex could reply, Felix said, "I'm patching this in to our air medic division. They can get a chopper over to that spot in a few minutes. We'll get him out of there and to a hospital in a hurry. You want me to call you back?"

"No, I'll wait until you have something." She couldn't hold back the tears that streamed down her face as she prayed silently.

Alex could hear Felix giving someone instructions on the radio, then he came back to her and said, "Hey, babe, let me call you back. I'm a little busy working with the air medic guys. I'll call you just as soon as I have something to report."

After Felix disconnected, Alex continued to pray silently. She felt absolutely helpless waiting for Felix to call back, dreading what he might have to report. The waitress returned, but she waved her away, interested only in having her prayers answered.

When her cell phone rang, she jumped as if electric current had passed through her body. It was Felix. She tried to control her anxiety and said, "How is he? Is he ..."

"You can relax, Alex. He's pretty banged up, but it looks like he'll pull through. Some internal injuries and a fractured shoulder, plus a bunch of cuts and bruises. But he's on his way to St. Luke's, the best trauma center in the area. He'll be in good hands, I promise."

Alex breathed a deep sigh of relief. It was as if a heavy burden had been lifted from her shoulders. She wasn't much of a church-goer, but her belief in the power of prayer had been restored.

Alex thanked Felix for all he'd done and requested the location of St. Luke's. She was halfway to her car when she remembered she'd forgotten to pay the waitress. She ran back inside, left a generous tip on the table, and headed to St. Luke's at top speed.

CHAPTER 24

A few minutes before noon, I finished what I was doing and called Joe Butler. In less than two minutes he was at my door with the usual wide grin on his face.

"Where to?" he asked.

I gave him the address and a curious look came across his face. "I'm surprised you know about this place."

"Why is that?"

His grin grew even wider. "Oh, it's sort of a local favorite and we try to keep it to ourselves."

By that I supposed he meant that it was a cop hangout, but I didn't bother to tell him how I knew about the place, or that I was meeting Ray and Alex. I was more convinced than ever that I needed to avoid sharing any information about the involvement of Ray and Alex in my investigation. If my life was in danger, theirs might be as well.

We retrieved Joe's car from the police garage and headed west, away from downtown. I was a bit surprised because I had the impression that my intended destination was the other direction.

When I asked Joe about this, he said, "Don't worry, Sheriff Harrison, we'll get there on time."

But in a few minutes, I was convinced that we were definitely not headed for my planned rendezvous. When I told Joe my concern, his smile faded and was replaced by a cold, sinister stare.

"Joe, what the hell –" I started to say, but he cut me off.

"We have to make a slight detour, Sheriff Harrison," he said acidly, sending chills down my spine, then pulled over to the side of the road.

From behind me I felt the cold steel of a gun barrel pressed against the back of my neck and a familiar baritone voice said, "We've got someone who wants to see you, Sheriff."

Butler was now pointing his own Glock at me. "I'll be taking your cell phone, Clint. You won't need it where you're going."

With two guns pointing directly at me, I didn't have a choice. I reluctantly withdrew my phone from my jacket pocket and handed it to Butler. He stepped out of the car, dropped my cell to the ground, then smashed it with his heel.

Then the lights went out suddenly as something hard struck me on the back of my head.

* * *

When I came to, my head throbbed with pain. I had no idea how long I'd been out. I was in a damp, dark basement or cellar, lying at the bottom of a rickety wooden stairway. The air was heavy with the odor of decay, mildew, and something even more offensive. I was unable to move. A foul-smelling rag was stuffed in my mouth. My arms were tied behind my back, and my legs were bound tightly together. The only source of light came from beneath a door at the top of the stairs. I struggled to free myself, but the heavy rope binding my arms and legs was tied securely. I knew I wasn't going anywhere anytime soon. I heard the faint sounds of men's voices somewhere above me, but couldn't make out what they were saying.

I heard a loud, creaking sound as a door opened and a rush of warm air washed over me. In the dim light from above, I could see a very large man descending the stairs that groaned under his weight. I closed my eyes and feigned unconsciousness as the footsteps drew near, accompanied by heavy breathing. I nearly gagged at the rank odor of cigar smoke. A foot kicked me in my ribs, but I remained still.

The big man grunted, then retreated up the stairs. I heard his deep, baritone voice: "He's still out cold. I musta hit him harder than I thought."

I recognized the baritone voice as that of the same man I'd seen on the grainy videotape in the governor's office.

Another man laughed, then someone kicked the door shut and I was enveloped in semi-darkness, and could hear only muffled voices again.

As my eyes adjusted to the faint light, I surveyed my surroundings. The room was no more than ten – or twelve-foot square with concrete walls and a dirt floor. It was probably intended for storage, but it appeared empty except for a large metal cabinet standing against the opposing wall. In the far corner, I spotted the opening of an air duct that extended to the floor above. I pushed myself into a sitting position and used my legs for leverage to scoot toward the air vent. My efforts were rewarded by the distinct sound of men talking.

Baritone Voice was talking to another man. There seemed to be only two men in the room, but who were they?

I heard a cell phone ring, followed by a muffled conversation. Then the second man said, "The boss is on his way," and Baritone Voice grunted.

I was sickened with the realization that one of my captors was Joe Butler ... the man Captain Wilkins had assigned as my driver. And now I had to reconsider, What is Wilkins' role in this? Whose side is he on?

And then I wondered if Butler was responsible for the explosion and fire? That would explain how he'd arrived at the scene so soon after the exposition. Slowly, the cobwebs began to clear from my mind and some of the pieces of the puzzle were falling into place.

I blamed myself for misreading Butler. But what could possibly motivate a person with his credentials to go to the other side? And who else was involved? If Butler was part of the conspiracy, did that include Wilkins as well? Wilkins had been eager to have Joe assigned to me, and it made sense that he'd only give this assignment to someone he could trust. Maybe my first suspicion about Wilkins had been on target after all. And, if Wilkins was involved, how much higher in the organization of the CCPD did the corruption reach?

How had I missed the warning signs? Wilkins' insistence on having Joe assigned as my driver was obviously intended to keep track of my movement. The listening devices in my motel room were of top quality, exactly what a police department world use in its own investigations.

Our movements, and perhaps even our conversations, had probably been closely monitored. They were just waiting for the right time to step in and thwart our investigation.

Carelessness on my part had placed my own life – and perhaps those of Ray and Alex – in jeopardy. And I was now powerless to do anything about it.

CHAPTER 25

I heard the sound of a car engine outside, followed by a car door being closed. Chairs scraped the floor and a door opened. Someone entered and said, "You have him secured below?"

By this time, I shouldn't have been surprised at anything. But I couldn't believe my ears when I heard the voice of Commander Lance Underwood. Now it all started to make sense. Was this the "Boss," or was Wilkins yet to make an appearance? I strained to pick up the ensuing conversation.

Baritone Voice: "Yeah, Boss. You bet. He's still out though."

Underwood: "Good. What about his cell phone? It has a tracking device."

Butler: "All taken care of."

Underwood: "Excellent, He has caused us way too much trouble. But he will soon pay for his meddling."

Baritone Voice: "I'd like a shot at him myself, Boss."

Underwood: "I'm sure you would, Frankie. But I've promised that someone else."

Frankie growled his disappointment.

Underwood: "As it turns out, we are not the only people who were inconvenienced by Sheriff Harrison."

Butler: "What do you mean?"

Underwood: "It's come to my attention that a certain Carlos Ortega would very much like to have the pleasure of seeing to Mr. Harrison's demise."

Ortega's name caught me by surprise. What business could Underwood possibly have with Carlos Ortega?

Frankie: "Who's this guy Ortega? And what's he want with Harrison?"

Underwood: "It seems that Sheriff Harrison was responsible for breaking up a very lucrative business enterprise Mr. Ortega operated in Los Angeles."

Butler: "That sounds like Harrison."

Underwood: "And Sheriff Harrison was also responsible for Mr. Ortega landing in federal prison."

Butler: "Ouch. No wonder he wants to get his hands on him."

Underwood: "It is my understanding that Mr. Ortega is a very – shall we say – vengeful man. And that he will take great delight in teaching Sheriff Harrison the error of his ways."

The statement was followed by another round of laughter. My death was being discussed as casually as if they were talking about the weather.

Frankie: "Sounds to me like we're doin' this guy Ortega a favor. So, what do we get in return?"

Underwood: "Mr. Ortega is doing us a very big favor by taking Harrison off our hands so that we can go on with our business without further interference."

Frankie: "So we're just gonna turn Harrison over to this guy Ortega?"

Underwood: "Yes, I expect Mr. Ortega or one of his associates to be here soon."

Frankie mumbled something.

Underwood: "I know what you were hoping for, Frankie, but you'll just have to get your kicks some other way."

Butler: "He's right, Frankie. We're better off out of the picture on this one."

Underwood: "No question about it, Joe. We'll just let Mr. Ortega do our wet work for us."

Frankie: "I dunno, Boss. Seems like we oughta be gettin' somethin' more outa this deal."

Underwood: "Well, Frankie, as a matter of fact, I have arranged for a certain amount of reciprocity that should prove quite profitable."

Frankie: "Ressaprossey what?"

Butler: "It means we get something in return."

Frankie: "Oh yeah? Like what?"

Underwood: "Let's just say that Ortega has been kind enough to supply us with contacts south of the border that will provide us with a fresh supply of ... ah ... talent."

Butler: "Young, willing and able, I'll bet. More people to fill in as 'domestic workers?'"

Underwood: "Ortega has assured me that the talent he can supply will more than fulfill the rather unique demands of our clients."

Frankie: "Okay. I get the picture, Boss. But I still wish I was the one takin' care of Harrison."

The room upstairs grew deathly quiet and I was left alone with my thoughts, desperately trying to think of a way to escape the fate that awaited me.

CHAPTER 26

Alex arrived at St. Luke's in record time. Doing her best to maintain her composure, she asked a uniformed security guard for assistance. He directed her to an information desk where she was greeted by a friendly, matronly-looking woman, whose name tag identified her as Dorothy. Scanning a clipboard, Dorothy informed Alex that Mr. Montijo was in surgery.

"It might be a while, honey," Dorothy said, "but you can wait in the third-floor lounge. It's just outside the ER. And Doctor Estrada will look for you there when he has news about your friend."

Alex took the elevator to the third floor and followed the signs to the lounge. Felix, a slender, mid-fifties man with ruddy features and an unkempt shock of silver hair, was waiting for her and greeted her with open arms. She ran to him and asked, "Is there any word yet?"

Felix shook his head. "No, not yet. I think there are probably some internal injuries, so it may be a while before –"

Alex collapsed in his arms, feeling both relief and anxiety, thankful that Ray was still alive, albeit fighting for his life.

Alex sat down and tried to relax, while Felix went to get coffee from a vending machine. He returned and handed one to her. "You could probably use something a bit stronger, but it's the best I can do under the circumstances."

Alex laughed and accepted the coffee. She was relieved to have Felix there with her, as if together they might improve Ray's chances of surviving the ordeal. She sipped the coffee and sighed deeply, feeling the tension that gripped her body.

Felix touched her arm. "Try to relax, Alex. He'll come through this okay. I have a good feeling about it."

She took his hand in hers, grateful for the support. "I hope you're right, Felix. I don't want to lose my partner."

"You know, Alex, your quick action probably saved his life. If you hadn't called me. God only knows when that wreck would have been found."

"Thanks, Felix. I'm just graceful you were available. Otherwise, I don't know ..." Her voice trailed off and she shuddered involuntarily. He put his arm around her shoulders and drew her close, and she was strengthened by his presence.

Felix asked, "Any idea what Ray was doing up on that mountain road?"

Alex shook her head, sipped her coffee, and said, "No idea. We were supposed to be getting together at noon today." She was careful not to mention Clint Harrison or the case they were working. She'd known Felix for many years, but she respected the confidentiality of the work they were doing.

She excused herself and went to find the women's restroom. Once inside, she checked to make sure she was alone, then dialed Clint's number. Once again, no answer. She wondered if there was a connection between Ray's "accident" and her inability to reach Clint Harrison? She tried to think of what to do next, but nothing came to mind.

Alex returned to the lounge, trying to mask the waves of anxiety that gripped her. Felix eyed her carefully and said, "Is there a problem?"

"No," she replied weakly, "just concerned about Ray."

Felix wasn't convinced, but he didn't press it. "Look, Alex, I've got to get back to the office and complete the paperwork. Will you be alright?"

She assured him she'd be fine, then asked, "What about the accident report? Can you check on that for me? I just can't shake the feeling that there may have been foul play."

He eyed her quizzically. "Sure, Alex. I'll check with the State Patrol and let you know just as soon as I hear anything."

Rising to leave, he put his hand on her shoulder. "Is there anything else?"

She looked into his eyes and said, "No Felix. You've been great. I'll be fine. I'll just hang out here till I learn something about Ray's condition."

After Felix left, Alex knew of no one to call – no one to turn to – and felt hopelessly alone and helpless.

Minutes seemed to drag into hours until Alex was startled by a tall, African-American woman wearing green scrubs and a wide smile standing next to her. "Are you here about Ray Montijo?"

Alex jumped up and, fighting to control her worst fears, stammered, "Uh ... yeah ... I mean ... Yes."

The woman spoke with a melodic Caribbean accent, "I'm Doctor Jameson. And who might you be?"

Alex identified herself and her relationship to Ray, then asked, "How is he? Is he ...?"

Dr. Jameson frowned. "He's pretty banged up, I'm afraid. Some internal injuries, which we've taken care of, plus a broken collar bone and assorted cuts and bruises. However," she broke into a smile, "he looks like a pretty tough hombre and I think he'll be fine. But he'll be with us for a while."

Alex laughed involuntarily as a wave of relief wash over her, and she thanked God for answering her prayers.

Doctor Jameson asked, "Does he have any family nearby?"

Alex thought for a second, then replied, "Just his ex-wife, Estelle.

But I don't know if they're on speaking terms these days?"

"Well, if you want to let her know," Dr. Jameson replied, handing Alex a business card, "have her call the main number and give the receptionist his name. She'll put Estelle through to the nurse's station."

Dr. Jameson thanked Alex for her efforts and told her that it would be several hours before she'd be able to see Ray. "Why don't you come back in the morning? By then, he should be able to have visitors."

At that, Dr. Jameson left Alex alone with her thoughts. It was a huge relief to know that Ray would survive, but she was still worn out from all the worry and tension. She had no idea what to do next. She tried to reach Estelle, but got voicemail. Alex didn't want to leave a long, involved message explaining what happened, and decided to try again later.

Alex was deep in thought when a tall, slender man in a tailored blue business suit, and a serious look on his face approached her. He was accompanied by a tall, attractive African-American woman wearing combat boots, jeans, and a white blouse. She wore her long, dark hair tied up in a ponytail that peeped out from beneath a baseball cap bearing a state police logo.

The man asked, “Are you Alex?”

Before Alex could react, the man touched Alex’s shoulder reassuringly and said, “It’s okay. I’m Captain Lawrence Wilkins.”

CHAPTER 27

My situation seemed hopeless, but I had been in tough spots before, and I wasn't about to give up without a fight. Although I was unable to free myself from the ropes that bound my legs and arms, I was able to push myself along the dirty floor, searching for something – anything – that I could use as a cutting tool.

In the semi-darkness, I spotted a large plastic bag containing something very odorous. I scooted over to the bag and discovered it contained fertilizer. Ignoring the foul smell, I inspected the bag and discovered an old pair of work gloves and a small hand trowel inside. The trowel was rusty and covered with filth, but I realized it might be just be what I needed to free myself.

I pushed over the bag with my shoulder, allowing the contents to spill out, and the trowel tumbled to the floor, covered with the smelly compost. Turning my back to the bag, I was able to grasp the trowel with one hand and began to rub the blade across the rope that bound my hands.

It was slow going, as I had trouble grasping the trowel tight enough to cut through the heavy rope. I finally managed to force the handle into a small opening between the back of the locker and the wall with the blade extending out several inches. Once I was satisfied that the handle was securely lodged behind the locker, I was ready to get to work.

I turned so that, with difficulty, I was able to run the rope tying my hands along the exposed edge of the blade. Then, slowly, an inch or two at a time, I moved the rope across the blade, praying to God that time was on my side. Eventually, I was able to get into a slow, consistent rhythm, moving the rope back and force against the blade. Several times my hands slipped and the blade cut into my wrists, but I ignored the pain and kept at it, hoping to free myself before the arrival of Carlos Ortega.

After several minutes, I began to feel a few strands of the rope breaking away. I redoubled my efforts and soon felt more strands break. Finally, I had worked through enough of the rope to allow me to pull first one hand free, then the other. Exhausted from the exertion, I collapsed and tried to catch my breath and regain my strength. After a few seconds, I untied the rope binding my legs, while saying a quiet prayer to St. Francis for this small success. But my celebration was short-lived. I was not yet free. Any minute my captors would be turning me over to Ortega and his men. I wasted no time in planning my next move. I needed to figure out what to do when they eventually came to take me to my executioner. They would be armed, and the small hand trowel would be useless against men with guns.

From high above, I noticed a tiny glimmer of light that I hadn't seen before. Moving closer, I discovered a small window at ground level – about six feet above the floor – that had been boarded over from the inside with a sheet of half-inch plywood. My pulse quickened with the discovery of a possible escape route. But I needed to find a way to reach it, remove the plywood covering, and make my way through the small window – perhaps no more than 18 inches wide – without being discovered by my captors.

In the far corner, I spotted a packing crate that, upon close examination, I might be able to stand on to reach the window. I tested it and decided that it would support my weight without collapsing. Now I needed something I could use to pry the plywood away from the window frame. The small garden trowel I'd used to cut through the rope might be just what I needed to pry the sheet of plywood away from the window. Whatever I did, I needed to act quickly and silently.

I pushed the packing crate into position and boosted myself onto it, trying to remain silent so as not to alert my captors. I grabbed the trowel, then slowly pushed myself into a standing position, doing my best to maintain my balance. Finally, I was able to reach the window, which was then at shoulder height. I examined the piece of plywood and noted that it was held securely to the window frame by a series of nails around its perimeter. I moved my fingers along the edge and discovered a small crack where the plywood sheet was slightly warped, allowing me to press the trowel between it and the window frame.

I slowly worked the trowel into the narrow opening, praying that it wouldn't crack under the pressure, or make a loud noise. But it seemed sturdy enough and I applied even, steady pressure until I'd opened up a small gap between the plywood and the window fame. Working as quietly as possible, I moved the trowel along the gap, exerting pressure to widen the opening an inch or so at a time. To my relief, the wood began to separate from the widow frame. All the while, I could still hear voices coming from the room above. Despite my progress, my stomach was tied in knots, and I hoped desperately that I'd be able to make my escape in time.

After several minutes I was able to loosen the plywood enough to allow my fingers to grip it securely and pull it free. Once the plywood was removed, I had to find a way to open the window. It was secured at the top by a metal lever that was rusted solid. I tried with all the strength I could muster to move it, but it held tight. To gain better leverage, I inserted the trowel between the window lever and the window frame and pushed hard. Slowly, a fraction of an inch at a time, the lever began to move. After several more tries, I was able to loosen the lever enough to open the window slightly. I rested long enough to regain my strength, then redoubled my efforts to push open the window. Finally, it gave way grudgingly, and I was able to open it all the way. Now the question was whether the opening would be large enough for me to crawl through.

I grasped the edges of the window frame and began to pull myself up and through the opening. But I soon found that the space I'd opened was much smaller than I'd anticipated, and I futilely tried to wish away a few pounds. I pushed, then pulled, and the going was slow and painful as the window frame pinched in against my shoulders. The opening just wasn't wide enough. Finally, I decided to try something different. I reached one arm through the opening as far as it would go. Then I angled my body in such a way as to allow me to slip my other shoulder through the opening. Finally, with one last push I got my upper torso through, then pulled my lower body through until I was lying flat on rough pavement. I was bruised, bloody and exhausted, but grateful for my small victory. But I knew I was far from free.

CHAPTER 28

At the hospital, the appearance of Captain Lawrence Wilkins came as a shock to Alex. She knew who he was, but was unsure how to react. Alex wondered if he could be trusted.

Was he responsible for Ray's "accident". Did he know what happened to Clint? And who was the woman with him? Her heart raced as she considered all the possibilities. She said nothing, fearing the worst.

Wilkins saw the uncertainly in her eyes. "It's okay, Alex. We're on the same side, believe me."

The woman with him nodded and smiled, but said nothing.

Wilkins looked around. "Let's see if we can find someplace a bit more private," and motioned for Alex to follow him. She did so reluctancly, and the woman brought up the rear. Wilkins ushered both women into an unoccupied office at the end of the hall, and closed the door behind them.

Wilkins gestured to the chair. "Please have a seat, Alex."

She did so reluctantly, while Wilkins and the woman remained standing. Despite Wilkins' assurance, she found it difficult to control her anxiety, wondering if she was about to be arrested.

Wilkins motioned to the other woman. "Alex, this is Loren Anderson. She's the supervising agent with a state-federal task force that has been investigating the illegal importation of young men and women into this country from Central and South America."

Loren flashed Alex a broad smile and sat down next to her.

Wilkins took a seat across from Alex. "I know you're pretty stressed out right now, Alex, but I need you to relax. Loren and I will explain everything."

Alex nodded cautiously, and Wilkins continued, "We don't have much time, so I'll let Loren fill you in."

Loren looked into Alex's eyes and began her story. "Our task force has been investigating human trafficking in the state for the last six months. We've determined that a very powerful cartel, located in Central America, is responsible for most of the human trafficking into the U. S. The victims are forced into prostitution, child pornography, and other vices."

As Alex listened intently, Loren revealed the details of the sinister operation, and the apprehension she'd felt earlier waned. But she couldn't help wondering what it had to do with the investigation in which, Clint, Ray and herself were involved.

At this point, Captain Wilkins interjected, "You see, Alex, I was very well aware of what you, Ray Montijo and Sheriff Harrison were up to." He saw doubt in Alex's eyes. "Let's just say I have some sources very high in the state government and leave it at that."

Loren resumed, "Your investigation could not have come at a better time, Alex. We've known for some time about the trafficking of persons going on here in the state. But we ran into a stone wall trying to get enough solid leads to find out who was behind it."

Wilkins said, "We had reason to believe that this activity was being conducted with help from inside our own police department. But we lacked any direct evidence to support our theory – at least until now."

Loren explained, "Your investigation was just what we needed to break something loose. It was the spark that ignited the fire. When that happened, all the pieces started falling into place."

Wilkins said gravely, "Unfortunately, Ray Montijo nearly paid with his life, Donna Sanders was murdered, and Sheriff Harrison's fate is still unknown."

Upon hearing this, Alex's anxiety returned. "I've been trying to reach Clint, but – "

Captain Wilkins said gravely, "We think he's been taken by the people you've been investigating."

"Oh my God," Alex replied, her eyes wide with fear.

Just then, Loren's cell phone chimed. She tapped the screen, then answered, "Anderson." She listened intently to a voice on the other end. "Roger that," she replied. "We're on our way."

Loren jumped up and motioned for Wilkins and Alex to follow, saying only, "We've got work to do."

The excitement in her voice was contagious. Alex and Wilkins hurried to keep up, and Alex silently prayed for Clint's safety.

CHAPTER 29

Loren, Alex and Wilkins exited the hospital at a half-run and got into a black Ford 150 SSV parked just outside the emergency entrance. Loren took the wheel while Wilkins got into the front seat and Alex climbed into the rear. In seconds, Loren had the car racing out of the circular drive at a breakneck speed. Neither Wilkins nor Alex spoke, and could only guess where they were headed or what was about to take place. As she drove, Loren used a Bluetooth device to carry on a rapid-fire conversation with someone. The roar of the engine and the din of passing traffic made it impossible for either Alex or Captain Wilkins to follow the conversation.

Finally, Loren disconnected, then said, "We're headed to a location on the south side of the city. We believe that Sheriff Harrison was forcibly taken by unknown persons. We have an assault team in place and are preparing to make entry."

Within minutes, they arrived at an abandoned gas station and convenience store located in a part of the city devoted primarily to manufacturing and warehousing. Loren drove to the rear of the building and brought the car to a screeching halt near a half-dozen other vehicles that bore the distinct look of unmarked police cars. She jumped out and motioned for Alex and Wilkins to follow her. Loren strode purposely to a large mobile command vehicle, opened the door and entered, with Alex and Wilkins close behind. Inside, several men and women were crowded around a large table covered with maps, blueprints and schematic drawings. They were dressed in military-like fatigues, bulletproof vests, and helmets, and were armed with assault weapons, both rifles and sidearms.

The mobile command vehicle was equipped with an assortment of high-tech monitors illustrating various views of an area situated at the end of the street, about 100 yards distant. Loren introduced Captain Wilkins and Alex to those in the command vehicle, then said, "Sheriff Harrison's team has been conducting a parallel investigation of alleged illegal activity inside the Capitol City Police Department."

This was followed by a chorus of murmurs of interest from the others.

Alex and Wilkins stood by while Loren provided an overview of the situation. She rolled out a site plan showing a large complex containing a few surrounding buildings of various types and sizes.

"This is the former site of a tomato processing and canning company. We believe all of the buildings are vacant except this one." She gestured to a small structure near the rear of the complex, then looked up at one of the monitors. "At one time this was the residence of the plant manager. As you can see, it has two floors, with an office on the first floor. There is also an attached garage at the rear. According to the building plan, there's a cellar below the office." She gestured to the office displayed on the monitor and said, "This is our objective. The entire complex is surrounded by an eight-foot chain link fence topped by concertina wire. There are several security cameras positioned at strategic locations around the building."

Loren turned to a large, burly man with a crew cut and chiseled features. "This is Lieutenant Tom Dooley, the team leader. He'll go over the details with you."

Dooley stood ramrod straight; his steel-grey eyes conveyed an air of self-assurance and command authority.

Before Lieutenant Dooley speak, someone said, "That's a lot of security for an abandoned building."

Dooley nodded. "We believe the hostiles have been using this building to conduct their illegal activities for some time. It's likely Sheriff Harrison is being held captive, and is in imminent danger. Therefore, immediate action is warranted."

Alex thought about Clint and shuddered involuntarily.

Lt. Dooley surveyed the others, then explained, "We are not sure, but it is possible that the abduction of Sheriff Harrison is tied in with our own investigation, and that those holding him may be the same ones we've been investigating."

Wilkins spoke up, "There is definitely a connection between the two investigations. There has already been one attempt on Harrison's life. Make no mistake, these are violent people we are dealing with. And," he said grimly, "we have reason to believe that we may have someone inside the police department working with this group."

Dooley pointed to one of the monitors that showed an aerial view of the area in question.

"We've had this site under surveillance for the last ninety minutes. Our thermal imaging system tells us that there are four persons inside the building." He indicated another monitor displaying blurred images of three persons, apparently sitting around a table. "This is a live feed of those inside the office. There is also one person in a cellar below it. We believe this is Harrison. To get to him, we have to take out those in the office."

A tall man with a ruddy complexion and a bushy mustache asked, "Is there another way into the cellar?"

Dooley shook his head. "Negative. Only through the office."

Loren passed around a photo of Harrison. "Be sure you don't mistake him for one of the bad guys."

Dooley pointed to another monitor. "The main entrance gate is electronically controlled and monitored by surveillance cameras."

As Alex listened to Dooley, she wished she could participate in the action that was about to take place, but she knew that was not possible. She'd just have to wait it out and pray for a successful outcome.

A stocky man with a full beard and dark, piercing eyes said, "With all that security, how do we make entry without being discovered?"

Dooley replied, "Good question." He turned to a young woman standing beside him. "This is Sergeant Samantha – Sammy – Collins. She's an advanced electronic countermeasures technician with the state police. She's our number one go-to person when it comes to overcoming electronic surveillance systems."

Sammy had azure blue eyes, rosy cheeks, a captivating smile, and a blonde ponytail that bounced to and fro as she spoke. With exacting precision, she explained, "They have a state-of-the-art security system. With video cameras and motion detectors at several locations around the building. That's in addition to the electrically-charged, 2000-volt concertina wire at the top of the chain link fence."

Someone whistled softly, perhaps expressing the view of several others in the group.

"But never fear," Samantha said with absolute confidence, "we've got it under control."

She held an electronic tablet that had a dazzling display of flashing lights and pulsing circuits that only she could understand.

"In just about ten minutes," Sammy said, glancing at her watch, "we will interrupt their security system just long enough for our assault team to cut through the fence and be prepared to make forcible entry into the building."

There were nods of approval, then Dooley said, "Okay, listen up. On my command, Sergeant Guzman," indicating a short Hispanic man with broad shoulders and a wide smile, "your Alpha Team will make entry by cutting through the fence at the rear of the complex." He pointed to the overhead view on the monitor. "From there, you'll make your way to the rear of the building. Take up a position there and be prepared to cut off any possible escape."

"Sergeant Chang," Dooley said, eyeing a slender Asian woman armed with a Glock 22 carried in a shoulder holster, "your Bravo Team will follow Alpha Team through the fence, then make forcible entry into the office using stun grenades. Hold your fire unless fired upon. We hope the element of surprise will allow us to gain control without firing a shot."

Lieutenant Chang said nothing, but gave a thumbs-up signal.

Loren and Wilkins exchanged glances. They were impressed with the overall planning and precision of the operation. Commander Long and Lt. Dooley appeared to have the situation well in hand.

Dooley checked his watch. "Okay, just under five minutes. Team leaders, let's make one last equipment and radio check, then proceed to your jump off location."

The two teams made one last check of their gear, then exited the command vehicle and climbed inside a large panel truck that would take them to the departure point.

Meanwhile, Alex, Loren, and Wilkins conversed quietly in nervous anticipation, watching the monitors and hoping for a successful conclusion of the assault.

At the designated time, Dooley told Sammy to cut the security circuit. But before she could react, they observed a shiny black, late-model Lincoln pull up at the gate. Dooley acted quickly, telling Sammy to hold off, and commanding Alpha and Bravo teams to remain in place, explaining, "We have visitors."

Dooley watched the monitor as the electronic gate opened and the vehicle pulled into the compound and parked in front of the office. A man emerged from inside, approached the car, and spoke to the driver. Then three men exited the Lincoln and followed the other man back inside.

Dooley spoke into this radio: "All teams, be advised. We now have three – repeat – three additional hostiles inside the office. They're all tough-looking Hispanic males wearing suits. But I don't think they're from the City's Welcome Wagon. Assume all inside the office are hostiles and probably armed. Proceed according to plan on my signal."

Two squawks on the radio indicated receipt of the transmission.

Dooley nodded to Sammy, who punched a series of commands into her electronic tablet, then said, "Their security system is down."

Dooley spoke into his radio again and gave the "go" order. Alex and Wilkins watched the monitors with breathless anticipation as the two teams, weapons at the ready, executed their assignments with military-like precision. Within seconds, both teams had made their entry.

Just as Bravo Team approached its objective, a loud staccato ringing sound filled the command vehicle, sending everyone inside into panic mode. Sammy turned to look at one of the monitors, then swore softly.

Instantly realizing what had happened, Lieutenant Dooley gave the alarm: "All teams, be advised. Their security system is back online. Your entry has been detected. Be prepared for armed resistance."

Tension in the command vehicle rose as they watched with apprehension, fearing the worst.

CHAPTER 30

After pulling myself through the window, I took cover behind a pile of oil large drums stacked alongside the outer wall and surveyed my surroundings. I discovered the position of the fading sun told me that I was on the west side of the building. The entrance and office were fifty feet to my right. To my left was a large attached garage. About 100 feet to my right was an electronically-controlled entrance gate.

The entire compound was surrounded by a ten-foot security fence topped by concertina wire. I spotted security cameras at several vantage points. I was betting that the perimeter was electronically monitored. For all I knew, it might also be supported by an electronic intrusion detection system. If so, it would be impossible for anyone to enter without being exposed. And getting out without being discovered would be equally difficult. I hunkered down to consider my options, and prayed for Divine guidance.

My thoughts were interrupted by the sound of the entrance gate opening. A sleek-looking SUV pulled in and drove to within 50 feet of where I hid. My pulse raced when I saw Carlos Ortega and two of his goons get out of the vehicle. Then someone exited the building and I heard Joe Butler greet the new arrivals. They followed him inside and I knew my escape would soon be discovered. I had no idea what to do next. The entrance gate had closed, and there was no way I'd be able to make it over the fence. My situation seemed just as hopeless as before, and time was running out.

I gaped in surprise when several heavily-armed personnel in tactical gear positioned themselves at the rear of the building. Was I hallucinating – or had the calvary finally arrived? I felt a surge of relief wash over me, but it was short-lived. A loud klaxon sounded the alarm, and I realized my rescuers had been detected. My jubilation was replaced by a feeling of dread. Without the element of surprise, my rescuers were vulnerable to fire from inside the building, and I could do nothing to help them. I had no choice but to remain where I was, hidden from view, and hoping for the best.

The assault force split into two teams. One headed to the opposite side of the building, while the other approached the front office and immediately came under automatic weapons fire from inside. They returned fire, but had no visible targets, and were themselves exposed. Then one member of the team fired a smoke grenade that crashed through a window into the office. Clouds of white smoke poured out through the broken window, temporarily halting the fire from inside. Two members of the assault team ran to the office door and prepared to make forcible entry. As they approached, the front door was thrown open and someone inside fired a shotgun blast that cut down one of the advancing officers, who fell to the ground with a severe leg wound. The second officer was hit by automatic weapons fire, and collapsed, blood seeping from a gaping wound on his shoulder. Two more team members rushed up to pull the wounded men to safety. The sound of splintering wood and loud shouts told me the second assault team was forcing entry from the opposite side of the building.

Then I spotted a figure dart from a door to my left and run into the garage. In seconds, the garage door was raised and a black Lincoln Town Car roared out, heading for the electronic gate. The driver was Lance Underwood. My heart sank as I realized that Underwood was about to make his escape. But to get to the gate, he would pass right by me. Somehow, I had to stop him.

In desperation, I pushed one of the oil drums directly into his path. It wasn't enough to stop him, but it did force him to veer away and slow down. That was all I needed to make my move. As he was about to pass by, I threw myself onto the hood of his car, and frantically dug my fingers into the gap between the car's hood and the windshield. I held on tightly as Underwood accelerated, trying frantically to open the entrance gate. As we approached, the gate was not fully open, but that didn't stop Underwood. Seeing what was coming, I braced myself for the crash.

We hit the partially open gate with a jarring crash, knocking the gate off its hinges. The impact jolted me, and it was all I could do to hold on. A round metal fence post ball flew by, barely missing my head. I ducked at the last second and struggled to get a better grip, but my fingers were being strained to the breaking point. It was only a matter of time before I'd be thrown from the rabidly-accelerating car. My body partially blocked Underwood's view, and I hoped this would slow him down, but it didn't deter him. He was determined to escape at all cost.

We approached a busy intersection, but Underwood couldn't see around me and sped straight through, barely missing several oncoming cars. I panicked when I spotted a large truck beginning to make a left turn in front of us. At the last second, Underwood spotted the truck. Too late, he tried to brake and turn to avoid the collision. The rapid deceleration of the car caused me to lose my grip, and I was thrown free a split-second before the deafening collision. I landed with such force that waves of excruciating pain shot through my body, and blood seeped from a large cut on my arm. I looked up to see the heavy truck collide headfirst into Underwood's car. The bone-jarring crash was accompanied by the sound of grinding metal, screeching tires, hissing steam, and shattered glass flying in all directions.

In seconds, the ruptured fuel tank of Underwood's car ignited and flames began enveloping the car. I could see Underwood inside, frantically trying to free himself from the deployed airbag, about to be immolated by the searing flames. At the last second, Underwood succeeded in forcing open the heavily damaged driver's door and crawled out, seconds ahead of the encroaching fire. He was alive, but severely injured. Blood streamed from an open wound on his head and he limped badly.

He spotted me lying helplessly in the street and stumbled toward me, staring at me with cold, savage hatred. As Underwood drew near, he pulled his revolver from a side holster and leveled it on me. I struggled to get to my feet, but was unable to do so. He was about to exact his own brand of justice for my interference.

He stood over me as blood streamed down his face, partially clouding his vision. His voice cracked in pained rage, "So, the mighty Sheriff Harrison finally gets what's coming to him. Mr. Ortega paid handsomely for the opportunity to deal with you himself, but now the pleasure is all mine."

A thousand thoughts flashed through my mind as his finger tightened on the trigger. At the last instant, I twisted my body to one side. The gunshot blast was deadening, and the heat of the discharge singed the side of my face. In frustration, he staggered forward and prepared to fire again. I arched my back and kicked savagely at him, landing a sharp blow to his knee, and heard the unmistakable sound of bone breaking. He howled in pain and fury, and collapsed atop me, cursing angrily. I grabbed for his gun and tried desperately to wrest it from his grasp, but he was stronger than me, and he held on tightly.

He tried to get to his feet, but I held on with all the strength I could muster. We were locked in a deadly embrace, both of us struggling for control of the gun. He pounded furiously at me with his free fist. I clung tightly to his gun hand, while he attempted to get a clear shot at me. I tried to get enough leverage with my legs to roll out from beneath him, but he had the advantage of both weight and muscle.

Blood from his head wound continued to pour down his face, and onto me. I could feel his hot, gasping breath on my cheek. Despite his injuries, he battled savagely. We both knew that only one of us would survive the ordeal. In one last-ditch effort, I attempted to push him off me. My strength gone, I lost my grip on the gun, and feared the worst. I heard a muffled explosion, and scalding pain shot through my side. I fell into a whirling vortex of darkness, and I knew that our life and death struggle was over, and I had lost.

CHAPTER 31

I came to in excruciating pain. The throbbing in my side and head told me that I was hurt, and the IV tube in my arm, and the steady pulsing of the nearby monitor, told me I was in a hospital bed. The motherly-looking nurse prodding and poking at me confirmed this assessment. The memory of Underwood's flight, my attempt to stop him, and our life-and-death struggle slowly emerged through a fuzzy haze in my mind. I shuddered, realizing how lucky I was to have survived, after all.

"Well, good afternoon, Mr. Harrison," the nurse said, in a friendly, upbeat voice. "It's nice to see you back among the living. I'm Abigail, your nurse." Her warm smile and amiable attitude were comforting, but did nothing to ease the throbbing pain coursing through my body.

I tried to rise, but the motion sent more pain racing down my side, and I gave up.

"Now you just rest easy, Mr. Harrison," Nurse Abigail said politely. "You're pretty banged up and you won't be going anywhere for a while yet." She checked the bedside monitor and noted something on a clipboard.

"I feel like I was run over by a freight train," I said wearily.

Nurse Abigail looked up from her clipboard with a bemused smile.

"Not far from it. I'm told you got thrown from the hood of a car just before it was hit head-on by a Mac truck. If that isn't enough, you were shot, suffered a concussion, sustained a few broken ribs and a broken wrist. The fact that you survived at all is a bit of a miracle, I'd say." She shook her head and turned to leave. "I'll let Doctor Stone know you're awake," she said on her way out. "He'll be in to see you shortly."

Left alone with my thoughts, the enormity of my near-death experience swept over me, and I knew I was fortunate to be alive. Then my thoughts drifted to Lance Underwood. Did he survive? And perhaps escape? What turned Underwood – a rising star in the police department – into a criminal? It was impossible to comprehend. And what about Joe Butler? The man Wilkins assigned to be my chauffeur had been perfectly willing to turn me over to Carlos Ortega, knowing full well the fate that awaited me. I could only blame myself for misreading these men.

My reverie was interrupted by a familiar voice: "Are you up for visitors?" I turned to see Alex Arrowsmith enter the room, followed by Captain Wilkins, and a tall African-American woman I didn't recognize.

Captain Wilkins smiled and said, "You gave us quite a scare, Clint."

Alex chimed in, but she wasn't smiling. "What were you thinking when you jumped onto Underwood's car? You could have been killed."

She was right and I knew it. In retrospect, I should have just waited for the assault team to do what they're trained to do. But that's not in my DNA.

"I know it seems foolish now," I said with only a hint of remorse. "But the thought of Underwood escaping was too much for me to bear. I had to try to stop him."

"Well," Alex said grimly, "you stopped him all right. Thank God you're alive to talk about it."

I couldn't argue with that. But then I wondered how they had located me since Butler had smashed my cell phone.

Captain Wilkins must have been reading my thoughts. He said, "I can fill you in on a few things, Clint."

"Please do," I answered.

Wilkins went on to explain that he'd been unable to reach Butler on his cell phone, and became suspicious when he learned that Joe had supposedly taken me to a restaurant, but neither of us arrived.

He went on, "We located Butler using the GPS tracker on his phone at the abandoned warehouse. By then, I knew we had a serious problem and I notified Loren."

"And what about Underwood? I hope you have him in custody." "In a manner of speaking, Clint," Captain Wilkins grinned. "Let's just say he's been put out of commission – permanently."

That sounded ominous, but I wanted to know the whole story. "So, what happened?"

Wilkins explained, "Two SWAT officers had set up an outer perimeter on the warehouse. When Underwood crashed through the gate, they took up pursuit, but were well behind. They arrived on the crash scene to see you and Underwood wrestling on the ground, but didn't have a clear shot. Before they could stop him, he fired the shot that struck you in the side. They took up defensive positions and shouted for him to throw down his weapon. Instead, he fired on them and they returned fire. He took several rounds to the head and chest and went down. He was pronounced dead at the scene."

It was a sad end for an officer who could have had a great career ahead of him, but I couldn't find it in myself to feel any regret. In the end, Underwood got what he deserved.

The African-American woman now stepped forward and extended her hand.

"Sheriff Harrison, I'm Loren Anderson. I'm with the state-federal task force. Maybe I can put this all into perspective."

"That would be great," I said, giving her a feeble handshake.

"Our team has been investigating a well-organized human trafficking ring that had been operating out of Capitol City for some time. We very recently discovered that Underwood and his crew have been using the Community Outreach Program as a cover to bring in undocumented women and children from Central America, with the promise of a good living and the 'American Dream'. But once here, they were forced into slavery or prostitution with threats to kill members of their family if they didn't cooperate."

I now realized the Community Outreach Program was the perfect cover for the operation.

Loren went on, "The good news is that we've rescued more than fifty women and children who were held captive and being manipulated by Underwood and his crew. And we think we'll probably find more as our investigation continues."

It was all too much to comprehend. I turned to Wilkins, "This whole thing started out because we suspected you were dirty. Did you know what we were actually up to?"

Wilkins gave a mild shrug. "No, not at first. But shortly before you arrived, I began to have my suspicions about Underwood, but there was nothing concrete I could prove. Apparently, Underwood must have guessed that I was getting close to exposing his operation. That's when he and Frankie doctored up that videotape to frame me, and sent it to the governor."

"But the frame-up backfired on him," I said, smiling.

"Yes, indeed it did," Wilkins said. "When Chief Ryan told me about the program audit, I figured it just might be a convenient way to look into Underwood's operation and throw the scent off me. But I thought it best not to tip my hand. I wanted to see what your investigation revealed."

"And all along we thought you were possibly dirty," I said, shaking my head.

"It may have been a mistake not to tell you right off about what we suspected," Wilkins admitted. "But I didn't expect Underwood to go to the lengths he did to keep his operation disguised. I thought it important that you be allowed to work without being influenced by our theories."

I had to admit that this made sense. But he had seriously underestimated Underwood's treachery.

"I also made a mistake in trusting Joe Butler to keep an eye on you," Wilkins confessed. "Butler was very clever. He had me fooled from the get-go. I had no idea he was in cahoots with Underwood."

I saw the remorse in his eyes, and was relieved to have been wrong about Wilkins. And I regretted that we'd both been wrong about Joe Butler.

Then, thinking about the thing that got me involved in the first place, I asked, "Did you know about the doctored videotape?"

"No," Wilkins replied. "After Underwood's death, we executed a search warrant for his home and office and recovered a great deal of incriminating items – including more copies of the videotape. I must say, it was pretty convincing."

"Indeed it was."

Wilkins went on, "We also found text messages between Underwood and Butler indicating that Underwood was aware of my suspicions about his operation. Apparently, Butler was Underwood's informant. And it was also Butler's idea to use the doctored videotape."

I put the rest together. "Underwood must have believed the tape would be enough to plant evidence of corruption on you. Then he and his crew could continue on with business as usual."

"That's about it," Captain Wilkins acknowledged. "But when your team started poking around, Underwood realized that you were getting way too close and could possibly stumble onto what they were doing."

"So, he had to find a way to shut us down," Alex injected.

"I guess the gas leak and exposition was no accident after all," I said wryly.

"Correct," Wilkins said. "That was most likely the work of either Joe Butler, or another of Underwood's associates – a guy by the name of Frank Giovanni, aka 'Big Frankie.'"

I flashed back to Donna Sanders. "I gather they were also responsible for Donna's murder."

Loren spoke up, "We too had our suspicions about what Underwood was up to before you arrived on the scene. Donna was working for us in an undercover capacity. She must have sensed that you were in danger and attempted to meet to warn you. Somehow, Underwood must have already been on to Donna, and took steps to eliminate her."

The thought of Donna dying at the hands of Underwood and his crew sickened me. I had known her for just a short time, but I would always remember her warm smile. I was deeply saddened as I thought about the caring woman who was just trying to do what was right.

"Hey, where's Ray?" I asked, suddenly realizing he was nowhere to be seen.

As if on cue, a familiar voice said, "Actually, we're neighbors, amigo. They got me right next door."

I turned my head to see Ray Montijo entering my room in a wheelchair, pushed by a nurse.

His head was covered with bandages and his arm was in a sling, but he sounded good. I let out a sign of relief while smiles broke out all around. But I was still puzzled by the enormity of it all.

I looked at Ray and joked, "So, you missed all the excitement."

Ray grinned. "Yeah, right. Our friend Underwood arranged for me to have a little 'accident.'"

"Actually," Loren said, turning to Ray, "your little 'accident' was carried out by the guy they called Big Frankie."

I thought about the vicious hit I'd taken to my head. Ah, Frankie..." I recalled Underwood saying his name when I was eavesdropping from below in the cellar, "I believe we've met."

Ray went on to describe his near-fatal crash and tumble down the mountain-side.

"My God, Ray," I exclaimed. "You're lucky to be alive!"

"Damn straight. By the grace of God and good old St. Christopher." Ray touched the St. Christopher medal he wore around his neck.

Loren Anderson filled me in on what had happened after Underwood's ill-fated escape attempt. "Two of my guys were badly wounded, but, thank God, they're going to live. Frankie went down with fatal wounds when the assault team made their entry. Two of Ortega's men, Manuel Rodiguez and Hector Lopez, were shot and killed as well."

"And what about Ortega?" I pressed. If that bastard had escaped again, Mary Alice and I still had targets on our backs.

"Carlos Ortega survived the shootout by using one of his crew as a human shield," Loren said, shaking her head in disgust. "You'll be happy to know he's now in the custody of U. S. Marshals, and he'll be extradited to Los Angeles where new federal charges await him."

Ortega's arrest was like a huge weight lifted off of me. I knew security around him going forward would be tripled this time.

"And Joe Butler?" I asked.

Wilkins looked pleased. "We have Joe in custody. I've been told that he's agreed to tell us all about their operation, including where we'll find more victims – in exchange for a plea deal."

"So, instead of life without parole, he'll probably get twenty years ... still not enough to suit me," Montijo scowled.

I couldn't agree with him more.

Doctor Stone arrived, introduced himself, and politely began ushering everyone out of the room, explaining, "I need to check Mr. Harrison's vital signs."

I thanked them all for coming, and for their part in taking down Underwood. I asked Alex and Ray to stay in touch, and they agreed to. We'd made a great team, and I was fortunate to have them working with me.

Doctor Stone proceeded to examine me, probing gently here and there, then made a few notations on my chart. "Well, Mr. Harrison, I'd say you're in remarkably good shape, considering what you've been through. With luck, you should be on your way home in a day or two. Do you have any questions for me?"

I had none, and he departed, leaving me alone with my thoughts. I sipped on some ice chips Nurse Abigail had left at my bedside, and reflected on the bizarre chain of events that I'd gone through. I thanked God that I'd survived. For the time being, this little corner of the world would be a bit safer now.

I knew I needed to place a long-overdue telephone call to Mary Alice. When was the last time we talked? I couldn't remember. But she must be worried sick by now, for sure. I tried to think of a good way to explain my failure to stay in touch, and to downplay the dangerous situation I'd been in. But I knew that anything but total honesty would be a waste of time. Sooner or later, one way or another, she'd find out what happened. Hopefully, she'd forgive me when she realized that my mission was a success, I was safe, and I'd be coming home soon. Her warm embrace and loving touch were just what I needed to ease my pain, buoy my spirits, and put this bizarre episode to rest.

www.ingramcontent.com/pod-product-compliance
Lightning Source LLC
LaVergne TN
LVHW020710110826
845149LV00012B/2197